There wasn't a single part of her body that did not ache for Shera's touch. Jamie wrapped her arms, thighs and even the tips of her toes around Shera, wanting to feel every inch of Shera's warmth against her own. She could smell the spicy aroma of Shera's perfume, feel the soft layers of Shera's hair falling across her breasts.

"I've wanted to do this for weeks," Shera said in a husky stammer. Shera teasingly thumbed Jamie's nipples, then took them one by one into her mouth. Jamie responded in writhing delight as the soft lips caressed each breast. In between the exhilarating moments of arousal, there were deep kisses and intimate glances that rocked Jamie's world.

Shera's tongue worked a slow, delirious magic between Jamie's legs. At the same time, with the forceful movement of her hips, Jamie drove Shera's fingers deeper into the wetness that betrayed her desire. A steep climb of pleasure, guided by a tenderness she had never known, ended in a wonderful release of love and passion

LOOKING FOR NAIAD?

Buy our books at
www.naiadpress.com

or call our toll-free number
1-800-533-1973

or by fax (24 hours a day)
1-850-539-9731

THE VERY THOUGHT OF YOU

EROTIC LOVE STORIES BY NAIAD PRESS AUTHORS

EDITED BY

BARBARA GRIER

AND

CHRISTINE CASSIDY

THE NAIAD PRESS, INC.
1999

Printed in the United States of America on acid-free paper
First Edition

Cover designer: Bonnie Liss (Phoenix Graphics)
Typesetter: Sandi Stancil

Library of Congress Cataloging-in-Publication Data

The very thought of you / edited by Barbara Grier and Christine Cassidy.
    p.   cm.
    ISBN 1-56280-250-X   (alk. paper)
    1. Lesbians—Social life and customs—Fiction.   2. Lesbians' writings, American.   3. Love stories, American.   I. Grier, Barbara, 1933 –   .   II. Cassidy, Christine.
PS648.L47V47   1999
813'.01089206643—dc21
                                                        98-48236
                                                          CIP

ABOUT THE EDITORS

Barbara Grier

Author, editor, bibliographer; writings include *The Lesbian in Literature, Lesbiana, The Lesbian's Home Journal, Lavender Herring,* and *Lesbian Lives,* as well as contributions to various anthologies, *The Lesbian Path* (Cruikshank) and *The Coming Out Stories* (Stanley and Wolfe). She is coeditor, with Katherine V. Forrest, of *The Erotic Naiad* (1992), *The Romantic Naiad* (1993), *The Mysterious Naiad* (1994). She coedited *The First Time Ever* (1995), *Dancing in the Dark,* (1996) *Lady Be Good* (1997) and *The Touch of Your Hand* (1998) with Christine Cassidy.

Her early career included working for sixteen years with the pioneer lesbian magazine *The Ladder.* For the last twenty-seven years she has been, together with Donna J. McBride, the guiding force behind THE NAIAD PRESS.

Articles about Barbara's and Donna's life are too numerous to list, but a good early overview can be found in *Heartwoman* by Sandy Boucher (New York: Harper, 1982).

She lives in Tallahassee, Florida.

Christine Cassidy

Since 1988, Christine Cassidy has been an editor for Naiad Press. She has worked in book and magazine publishing for nearly 20 years and is currently Marketing Director of PressCorps, Inc. For the past two years she has also done marketing and promotion for Fatale Video. From 1988 through 1998, she served as Director of Marketing and Circulation at Poets & Writers, Inc. She is a member of Webgrrls, the New York New Media Association, New York Advertising and Communications Association and the M.I.T. Enterprise Forum, and is the former co-coordinator of The Publishing Triangle.

With Barbara Grier she coedited *The Touch of Your Hand* (1998), *Lady Be Good* (1997), *Dancing in the Dark* (1996) and *The First Time Ever* (1995). Her work has appeared in several magazines and anthologies, including *The Persistent Desire: A Femme/ Butch Reader*, edited by Joan Nestle (Boston: Alyson, 1993), *The Lambda Book Report*, *Our World*, *Poets & Writers Magazine*, and *On Our Backs*, among others. She was the recipient of a New Jersey State Council on the Arts grant in poetry and has been a fellow at the MacDowell Colony in New Hampshire. She holds an M.F.A. in poetry from Columbia University and a B.A. from Sarah Lawrence College. She can be seen, courtesy of photographer Morgan Gwenwald, in *Butch/ Femme*, a lively collection of photos edited by M.C. Soares. Her first story for Naiad, "The Garden," appears herein.

She lives in New York City with Nan Kinney and may be reached at cccassidy@aol.com.

TABLE OF CONTENTS

One Hour

Laura Adams

Her hands are warm on my skin. I want to say her name, but I cannot waste time on words.

Her chin brushes the crook of my arm. I can hear the delicate sound of her breath leaving her body. Is she as drunk as I am at the arrival of our stolen hour?

My warmth flows to her in my gaze, a smooth passage of tenderness that she returns. We pour our love back and forth through the channel of our fingertips. I want to snap the hourglass in two to stop the flow of time, but then we would be separate. It would be unbearable.

I am as familiar with her body as I am with my own. More down covers her left forearm than her right. The small of her back is almost hot to the touch. When she is passionate her ears and toes redden. She can ice a room when she is cold.

She kisses me and I am overwhelmed with wanting her body, but I want more for this hour to never end. Would I give up the pleasure of her body if it meant I could be with her always? In a second.

When she is away, in her real life where I am only a memory to her, my thoughts turn in every idle moment to the next hour when we will join hands. She moves under me, draws my hand to her. I am in her, part of her. I try to stay in that moment, but I am already past it. I am already missing her.

We begin again. This time she is quick to roll me onto my back. I want to take her again, but I don't have any time to fight. She is between my legs with her mouth and her fingers and I surrender to the searing heat of it, the soft and hard of it. It takes many long minutes to satisfy her. I try not to feel them slipping by. My pleasure is intense, but I am already missing her.

I keep the hours by the length of her absence. When I am with her it is the minutes that matter.

My face in the pillows, I can smell the scent of her hair. Her fingers press into me, harder with my urging and harder still as I rise to meet her. My heart beats faster than the seconds passing. She keeps me on my stomach when I am spent, her hair tickling my shoulders, her breasts hard against my back.

I rest, for just a minute, then she gets up for a glass of water. When she is within reach I pull her back into the bed. We are just getting started and our time is almost gone.

Trite but true, sixty minutes to most lesbians is a quickie. It is all I will ever have with her.

The warmth of her is behind me. Her tongue traces the nape of my neck as her fingers reach again for my nipples. She strokes them to anticipation again, and I am falling into the well of her need. I feel whole.

I tell myself that I will not watch her dress, but when I should look away I can't. I watch her shoulders disappear into a blouse, her legs into sheer hose. I notice that her skirt waist is a little loose and her blouse buttons a little tight. Does he notice? I doubt it.

I am a therapist appointment. I am a lie. I am her indulgence. I am a stolen hour smothered into a lifetime of existence. The hour I yearn for has passed. I have one hundred and sixty-seven more to get through before I see her again.

These terms are unacceptable to me. They always have been. But I am yet again stretched out on a motel bed, steeped in her satisfaction, watching her dress.

Zip, snap, she is almost done. I sit up and wrap

the sheets around me like armor. It is time to be strong, but if I was strong I would not be here. Last week would have been the last time. Or the week before that, or the month, quarter, year before that.

The cheap clock on the bedside table flicks to a new hour. She picks up her keys.

At the very core of my being is a clock, keeping time by the ticks of atoms joining and the tocks of atoms coming apart.

Tick. "I love you." I mean it.

Tock. "I have to go," she says, as if that is an answer.

Four Letters
Julia Watts

January 3, 1946

Dear Marty,

This is just a note to say hello and to wish you a happy New Year. I hope this letter finds you healthy and happy. Things are good here. Quiet, but good. Of course, "quiet" is no surprise. You know how these little Kentucky towns are.

I was just thinking about that first day I walked into that plant in Chicago, scared because I had never held a real job before, and you were the first person I saw. I was kind of scared of you too, because I had never seen a girl that looked like you, with your short hair and those brogans on your feet the size of gunboats. But when you started talking I had to smile because you sounded just like me. I guess the difference between us is that I was always a little homesick for the Kentucky mountains, and you always said you'd rather die than go back home.

Well, now all I have to do if I want to see a mountain is look out my window. Bobby built me the cutest little house, but when I say "little," I do mean little. It's three rooms, one right behind the other, plus a bathroom. Everything about it is shiny and white and new. If I spill a drop of bacon grease on the stove, I have to mop it up right that second. If something's shiny and new, you feel like you have to keep it that way.

It's queer, though. This house is a lot bigger than my apartment in Chicago. You remember it, don't you? Just one room, and the bathtub was smack-dab in the middle of the floor, so I put a board over it to make it double as a kitchen table. This house is three whole rooms, but somehow it seems smaller than that funny little apartment. I guess it's because there's two of us living here. The other day Bobby asked me when was I gonna have a baby, and I said, "Where would we put it? In a dresser drawer?"

Married life is good. It just takes some getting used to. It's kind of funny that me and Bobby have been married more than two years, but we're just now getting to spend time together. We hadn't known each other but two weeks when we got married, and he got shipped off to the war the morning after our wedding night. We both would have waited a lot longer to marry if it hadn't been for the war, but Bobby said he couldn't stand the thought of dying in a foreign land without having made an honest woman out of me.

So now we're getting to know each other, getting used to what it's like to live with another person. Mama says I got spoiled in Chicago, living by myself and being able to have things the way I wanted them all the time.

How are things at the plant? Say hey to the girls for me, especially Pauline and Betty. I know it sounds crazy, but sometimes I miss factory life. Here, I get up every morning at five and fix Bobby's breakfast and pack him his dinner to take to the mines. After he leaves, there's not much to do but clean up the house, which is clean already, until it's time to cook supper. I'm not as tired at the end of the day as I was when I was working at the plant, but it sure is quiet. Mama says you wait till you have a passel of younguns and you'll wish you had that quiet again. She's probably right.

Well, I'd better wind up this letter. I think of you often and our fun days in the Windy City, but I have to say I don't miss January weather in Chicago one bit. Ha! Write me if you get the time and let me know how you are. A letter from a friend sure would brighten my day.

Yours truly,
Lois

January 19, 1946

Dear Marty,

I was so happy to get your letter today I just about danced a jig in front of the mailbox. But I was sorry to hear that you and the other girls lost your jobs in the plant. I understand why the boys want their old jobs now that they're back home, and I reckon they deserve them as hard as they fought for our country. But what you're saying makes sense too. A single girl has got to earn a living, since you've got no husband to take care of you. Anyway, I hope you end up liking your job at the grocery store, even if the pay's not as good as it was at the plant.

Not much is new here. More of the same, I guess. Cooking and cleaning don't make for much in the way of news. I guess the only news I have is that me and Bobby are trying to have a baby. He wants to be a daddy so bad he's about to pop. So it seems like most of the time I'm either standing on my feet in the kitchen or lying on my back in the bed. Ha! I can't believe I just wrote that, but I've always said crazy things to you I'd never say to anybody else.

Do you still go over to Rusty's Bar and Grill on Friday nights? Sometimes I think about that cold beer and those good, greasy hamburgers, and I can just taste them, you know? Except for the Hippodrome, which only changes pictures every two weeks, Morgan doesn't have anywhere to go of a night. Bobby goes off to shoot pool after supper sometimes, but that's just for the boys.

Several of us young wives get together one morning a week for coffee. It's not like the talks you and me and the girls used to have at Rusty's, though, where we'd laugh about work and make fun of our boss and talk about everything from politics to movie stars. All these wives talk about is how their little Johnny said so-and-so or their little Susie said such-and-such. Since I don't have a little Johnny or Susie yet, I don't have much to contribute. But since me and Bobby are trying to make a baby, that should change soon.

Well, I should probably sign off for now. Mama's coming over this afternoon. She's trying to teach me to sew, but it's not working. I've stuck myself with the needle so much I look like a human pincushion. Ha! I'll be looking forward to your next letter.

Yours truly,
Lois

March 23, 1946

Dear Marty,

I'm sorry it took me so long to answer your last letter. A lot of things have been happening, and it's been hard to find the time to sit down and write.

I guess some of your last letter took me by surprise, too. Not the part where you said you like girls — I had kind of figured that out. Even though I'm just an ignorant country girl, I notice what goes on between people, and I thought there was some-thing between you and Betty. I saw the way you looked at her, and I noticed that on nights when we went out drinking, you always volunteered to walk her home. I'm sorry you two don't see each other anymore. Betty's a real nice girl. So are you, and the fact that you like girls didn't shock me or bother me at all.

Now I'll tell you what did shock me. It was when you came right out and asked me, "Are you happy?" I know it doesn't sound shocking, but you know what? Nobody has ever asked me that question before. Not Bobby. Not Mama. Nobody. That's queer, ain't it? Three simple little words — are you happy? — and nobody's ever said them to me.

Don't get me wrong. I know Mama loves me, and Bobby loves what he knows of me. It's just that Mama has never thought much about being happy. She's always been too busy worrying about doing what she's supposed to do. She's the oldest of six brothers and sisters, and so she's been carrying a youngun on her hip practically from the time she could walk. She got married at sixteen and had my brother and sister and me and had to look after us with Daddy in the mines all day, which always worried her. When Bobby took his job in the mines, Mama said to me, "It ain't easy havin' a miner for a husband, Lois. Every day when he walks into that big dark hole, you wonder if he'll ever walk back out of it." It would never occur to Mama to ask me if I was happy.

And Bobby, it just wouldn't occur to him that I'd be anything other than happy. I've got a nice little house to look after and enough money to go to the show or buy a magazine when I feel like it, so why shouldn't I be happy? I guess Bobby just assumes I'm happy because I have what women are supposed to want. And to his thinking, all women want the same thing.

And so your letter made me think about whether or not I'm happy. And it kind of made me mad, too, because it was a question I didn't want to think about.

I told you about us trying to have a baby. Well, we'd been trying and trying night after night until it started to feel like we were trying to do something, instead of just doing something that was supposed to be fun. Finally Bobby told me I ought to go to the doctor because there must be something wrong with me.

Doc White here in town sent me to another doctor in Lexington for tests, and it turns out Bobby was right. There is something wrong with me. Tumors — they're not cancer or anything — but they grow in my womb, so there's no room for a baby. The tumors won't hurt me or make me sick; they just make me barren. The doctor who told me about them was real nice and held my hand. There were even tears in his eyes when he told me I couldn't have a baby.

But Marty, this is the awful part. This is the secret. I was glad.

Bobby didn't say a word all the way back from Lexington. His mouth was set in a tight little line, and he stared straight ahead at the road. I knew his heart was breaking, but I couldn't think of a thing to say to him. Back when he asked me to marry him he said he wanted a whole houseful of kids, and all his buddies at the mine are already daddies. I felt bad for Bobby, but I didn't feel bad for me.

The truth is, I felt good. Don't get me wrong. I like kids fine. When my sister brings hers over to the house, I'm always glad to see them come. But they're always loud and into everything, and by the time the visit's over, I'm glad to see them go. I think I was scared of having kids of my own — kids I couldn't send packing when they gave me a headache. I could never explain this to Bobby because women are supposed to want children. And what do you do when you've up and married a girl who doesn't want the things she's supposed to want?

That's the reason your question bothered me so much, Marty. It's like you looked right into my soul. I haven't been happy. I've been trying to be happy, but you can't make happiness by trying, not any more than you can make a baby when you're barren.

Bobby is good to me, even now when I know I'm a big disappointment to him. He's good to me, but he doesn't know me. Him and me have never had long talks like you and me used to have. He'd never think to talk to me like that. He's too caught up in his being a man and my being a woman. And he'd never understand how a woman could get more satisfaction out of making airplane parts in a factory than out of making soup beans in a kitchen.

I miss you, Marty. I miss our talks, and I miss earning my own money. Even though I never thought it would happen, I'm starting to miss the Chicago skyline the way I used to miss the Kentucky mountains. I guess home is where you're happy, and that doesn't have to be where you're from.

But I've cast my lot here. Mama says I should be thankful that Bobby didn't throw me out of the house for being barren, and she's right. She says a woman should be thankful for what she's got, and I'm trying to be. If I can't be happy, I can at least be thankful. But Marty, I am both happy and thankful to have a friend like you.

Yours truly,
Lois

April 28, 1946

Dear Marty,

You probably noticed my change of address on the envelope. I'm staying at my sister's right now, which, thank the Lord, is just a temporary thing until the divorce is final. I know your jaw just hit the floor. Don't worry. I'm about to explain.

After we got the news from the doctor in Lexington, Bobby started going out of an evening. I figured my being barren drove him to drink, and it had, but that wasn't the only thing it drove him to do. There's this trashy bottle-blonde that works at the dime store, and she's already missed her period, even though her and Bobby haven't been seeing each other but six weeks. Between you and me, I wonder if the baby's his, but he's happy so I'm keeping my mouth shut.

When he told me he was leaving me for her, I pretended to cry a little so he wouldn't feel bad, but my little heart was flapping in my chest like a butterfly because I knew I was free. I wish the two of them happiness and more babies than you can shake a stick at.

Now, I guess, is the moment of truth. Did you

really mean it when you said if I ever wanted to come back to Chicago, I could stay with you till I found a place and a job? I reckon you did mean it. You don't tend to say things you don't mean.

About that question you asked me ... How much do I remember about that night when you came over to my apartment drunk after you and Betty had been fighting? Well, I think I remember everything. I made you coffee, and you sat on the couch with me and told me how I was your best friend and you liked me so much and you hoped my husband knew how to treat me right. I said Bobby was a good man, and you took a little flask out of your jacket pocket and poured some of what was in it into your coffee.

I never will forget the way you looked at me. Men have looked at me before like they're looking through my clothes, but you looked at me like you were looking through my skin, looking right inside of my heart. Maybe you were looking to see whether or not I loved Bobby. The answer was written on my heart, all right, and the answer was no. I think you knew that before I did.

But I guess what you really want to know is, do I remember when you kissed me? I do. It was a warm, dizzying kiss — warm and dizzying like the whiskey you'd been drinking. And I remember I kissed you back for a couple of minutes — kissed you back and liked it till a voice in my head said, *Stop. You can't do this. This is a woman you're kissing.* And that's when you pulled back and said you were sorry, you were drunk, and you didn't usually kiss girls like that. I think we both knew better.

Marty, I think if you was to kiss me like that

again, I'd tell that little voice in my head to shut the hell up.

I've tried to do the right thing, or to do what other people have told me is the right thing. I've tried being a nice married lady, and it's left me numb and hollow. Now I'm about to be a divorcee, and I don't give a good goddamn what anybody thinks about me. I want to find a new way of living my life, and I'm willing to give what we almost had in Chicago a try.

But get this straight. I'm not gonna be your little housewife. Once I get a job in the city, I want my own place, even if it's just a one-room apartment with a bathtub in the middle of it. But if you'd like to come over for supper some evenings, I'd like that. And if you'd like to stick around for breakfast the next morning sometimes, I'd like that, too.

I'll wire you when the divorce is final. As soon as the papers are signed, I'll be coming home.

Yours truly,
Lois

Fair Play

Barbara Johnson

I couldn't believe I let my sister talk me into going to the York County Fair. A city girl myself, the idea of hanging around with thousands of rural country types and their cows had no real appeal. Still, it had been a couple of months since we'd seen each other, and my niece pleaded so plaintively that I agreed to drive up from Washington, D.C., for a visit.

For starters, it was a hot miserable day. Never one to enjoy the humid summers of D.C., I liked even less walking around acres of baking tarmac. It actually turned out that the only place to really get out of the sun was the long sheds that housed the various farm animals. I quickly became very friendly with a black Angus cow named Cinder.

Plus, I'd never seen or heard such a cacophony of confusion and noise and smells. There were booths and exhibits galore selling everything from lemonade to hot tubs. One area contained rides and games of every imaginable sort, every one of them a rip-off. And of course, one can't leave out the top attraction of these things: the freak show. I have to admit, I did go in with my sister. The show was actually nothing but a bunch of faded photographs, poorly made mannequins, ratty old stuffed animals with two heads, and jars full of mysterious objects that I didn't want to examine too closely. All in all, it was a rather pathetic look at the past lives of creatures and people once exploited for their differences. The only so-called freaks here today were the old dwarf who took my ticket and the four-hundred-pound man who slumped in his chair in the interminable heat. Shirtless, he read a *Superman* comic book and waited for people to drop dollars into a bucket at his feet.

After following the family around and eating more junk food in three hours than I'd eaten all year, I pleaded a sun-induced headache and watched them merrily go off to the kiddie rides. I bought another ice-cold lemonade and headed over to the game booths. It was always fun to wander through and watch people losing their money on a quest for gigantic red dogs or the latest Beanie Baby. I'd even been known to drop a dollar or two myself.

Truth be known, I was really on the prowl, looking for a gay person, any gay person. This much happy heterosexuality was more than I could take in a day. It had also been a number of weeks since I'd last been out with a woman, and I could tell my libido was kicking into overdrive. The trouble was, most of the women in this part of the country all looked like dykes, at least the kind I liked. Short hair, jeans, boots and no-nonsense shirts seemed to be the norm. Occasionally, I'd see a halter top or two and bangs that could rival any tidal wave. On the whole, I probably had the longest hair of anyone there, excluding a couple of men. And I'm sure my powder-blue shorts set and white Keds made me stand out like a rabbit in a cabbage patch.

So, I wandered up and down the aisles, sometimes admiring the prizes, but most times wondering where they found all this junk. The hardest game, by my reckoning, was pool. For two dollars you got four colored balls, plus the cue ball. Pocket all four balls and you won a little stuffed husky. Miss even one, and that was the end of the game. With each win, you could trade your husky in for the next larger size. The grand prize was a white buffalo that stood about four feet tall and would take at least two people to carry. You had to trade in three jumbo huskies to get that one, and it took eight games to get the jumbo.

I stood in the meager shade of the canopy near the top left of the pool table and watched four men each drop several dollars. Sometimes they won, but most times they didn't. Perhaps having me standing there watching made their male egos unable to accept defeat. All I know is, the concession person kept grinning my way with each loss.

I soon tired of watching and was about to walk away when a woman strode purposefully up to the table, dollar bills ready. She wore the requisite costume of blue jeans, boots and white cotton shirt — hers sleeveless — but her attitude was somehow different from all the other women at the fair. She caught my eye and winked. I was smitten. Her eyes were as blue as a summer sky, but her short hair was as black and smooth as a raven's wing. Her jeans were obviously new, and from the stares of the men behind her, she filled them out pretty nicely too.

She leaned across the table and lined her cue ball up very deliberately. The open collar of her shirt formed a vee that dipped sensuously toward full breasts. I caught an enticing glimpse of cleavage, and then she sent the white ball smacking into the group of four. They scattered, one plopping immediately into the top right corner pocket. She smiled and took her next shot. The ball fell into the middle left pocket. She walked in my direction.

" 'Scuse me," she said, her low voice rolling over me like an ocean wave. I felt my heart beat faster and a fluttering begin in my stomach. She leaned over the table, her ass in those tight jeans beckoning me. I could literally feel my mouth water.

She stood and watched the remaining two balls both fall into different pockets. Before any of the men could pull out their money, she held up two more dollars. The concession person started to hand her the smallest husky, but she shook her head. She made short work of the next four balls, and then the next four. Before she started on game four, she looked right at me.

"What size doggie would you like?" she asked with a provocative grin that made me tremble.

I wanted the biggest one, but she was five games away from that. The four men and the concession person all looked at me. She still stood watching me expectantly. I had to say something but couldn't. Instead, I pointed to the jumbo size.

"You don't want that cute little buffalo over there?" she asked with a toss of her head.

I could feel my cheeks burning. I had six pairs of eyes on me. If I said yes, would she keep throwing money down? It would cost her forty-eight dollars to trade up for the buffalo, and that was only if she never lost a game. If I said no, would she be insulted? I shook my head. She laughed and turned her attention to the new game, ignoring the four men who kind of danced around behind her. They were torn, I'm sure, between admiring her skill with the pool cue and wanting to soothe their bruised male egos by beating her at the game. I saw their hunger as their gazes raked over her lean, strong body.

It seemed like only seconds passed before the concession person was placing an oversized stuffed dog in my arms. The woman stood next to me. I had to look up at her, she was so tall. Her blue eyes danced with laughter, and her rosy lips beckoned me like a butterfly to nectar.

"Hey, girl!" The man's voice grated harshly into my thoughts. "How 'bout a challenge game?"

"Next time, fellas. I'm gonna take my little friend here out for a lemonade."

She put her hand on my elbow and guided me out into the sunshine. I blinked but couldn't put my sunglasses on, the dog in my arms was so big. She slid the glasses off the top of my head and over my eyes. Her touch made the hairs on my neck stand on end. I felt my scalp tingling.

"Thank you so much," I managed to say finally. "This was awfully nice of you."

"Well," she drawled, "so you *can* talk. I was beginnin' to think you were mute. What's your name?"

"Claire."

"Claire." She repeated my name like I was some long-lost lover. She smiled slowly. "I'm Amanda, but you can call me Mandy."

"You from around here?" was all I could manage.

"Originally, but I moved as soon as I graduated high school. Been livin' in southern Virginia. You?"

That would explain the accent that I couldn't quite place. She had a soft drawl, a cross between North and South with a bit of North Carolina influence. Quite pleasant, I surprised myself in thinking.

"I live in D.C. Just came up to visit my baby sister and her family."

I stumbled suddenly. The big unwieldy dog in my arms had blocked my view. Her hand shot out to steady me, and then she took the dog from me. I could feel the furious flush on my cheeks, but then the humorous glint in those incredible blue eyes made me forget my embarrassment. Her wide smile just about drove me crazy. I found myself wondering where the nearest hotel was and if I had my American Express card with me. She must have read my thoughts.

"Don't suppose you'd care to leave the fair? I'm stayin' just a short drive away." Her voice was low, suggestive.

"I think I'd best stick around here. I have to meet my sister in an hour." But I was feeling adventurous and smiled boldly back at her as I touched her arm, letting my nails run gently over her bare skin. "There must be somewhere around here a girl can have some privacy though."

I never expected Mandy to take my flirtatious suggestion seriously, but her blue eyes glittered as she grabbed my hand purposefully. She led me to one of the animal sheds, the one with the pet Vietnamese pot-bellied pigs. In my earlier wanderings, I had gone in there and marveled at how the pigs' owners had made the stalls into little living quarters. Yes, there was straw, but also miniature beds complete with sheets and blankets. One of them even had a television. The beasties also used litter boxes, like cats. I'd also noticed that one pig had the extravagance of two stalls, the wire windows of one completely covered with blankets so no one could see inside, and it was to this one that we went.

"Hold on one minute," Mandy said as she scooted inside the covered stall. A few squeals later, the pig darted into the uncovered one and stood glaring up at me, as if somehow blaming me for his eviction.

Mandy emerged seconds later and took my hand. I hesitated. She couldn't really be thinking what I thought she was, could she? She grinned and tugged my hand. "C'mon, sweet Claire," she said, slowly licking her lips. "We'll have complete privacy."

She must have seen the doubt in my face. "This

is my brother's pig," she explained. "He's already left for the day. No one comes in unauthorized."

"No one?"

She leaned in close to me. "Lends a bit of excitement, doesn't it?" Her lips brushed my neck.

I had to admit she was right. The thought of making love, practically in public, did make me shiver with the danger of it. Mandy tugged my hand again. This time I followed her, and she shut and locked the back door behind us. Unlike what I expected, there was no pungent animal smell, just fresh hay. She'd even spread a clean blanket over the hay. The little doorway between the two stalls was closed tight. Enclosed in blankets, the stall was dark with just enough light filtering in through the fabric. I felt like we were in a tent. She pulled me down into the hay.

Her kiss was soft and gentle at first, then more demanding. It had been so long since I'd been with a woman that I felt dizzy. Her strong hands held me firmly. With passionate urgency, we stripped off our clothes. Her body was hard, muscular. A swimmer myself, I knew my own body was firm. Kneeling together, we ran our hands down each other's bodies. I kissed her neck, tasting salt. She smelled so good.

We kissed and played with each other for what seemed like hours. I couldn't get enough of the feel of her — either her hands on me or mine on her. She finally leaned forward and pushed me down onto the blanket. The straw beneath it poked through, pricking me, but I forgot all that as her mouth blazed a warm, wet trail down my throat, chest and belly. I knew I was ready for her.

When her mouth made contact with my most

intimate spot, I gasped and fought to control the moan that rose in my throat. Somewhere in the red-hot haze of my need and want, I vaguely remembered that this was no private tent hidden deep in the woods. I pulled the blanket to me and held it tight against my mouth. With my other hand, I grasped Mandy's hair. With her tongue and fingers, she brought me to a place I'd not been in a long while.

It seemed as if I was floating above us. I could see her strong, firm back as she lay between my legs, see the movement of her shoulders and arms as she thrust her fingers deep inside me. Her head moved in rhythm, her hair dark and thick between my fingers.

I couldn't control the loud groan that escaped me as I shuddered into blissful release. I almost laughed out loud when I heard an answering grunt from our porcine neighbor. For a few minutes, I lay quietly, letting my breathing return to normal and feeling the blood rush warmly through my body. Mandy stayed between my legs, caressing my thighs until the sensation turned to tickling and I pulled her up.

I kissed her deeply, then urged her up until her thighs straddled my face. She braced her hands against the wall as I grabbed the twin globes of her firm ass and began to lick her clit, breathing in the musky scent of her. She was, oh, so wet. I'd not enjoyed the taste and smell of a woman in a very long time.

Mandy gasped suddenly and grabbed my head. I opened my eyes to look at her. Her head was thrown back, her tongue darting out to lick her lips. I closed my eyes once again and held her tight as her legs trembled against me. As her juices flowed into my mouth, I couldn't help but think of the refrain from that Cris Williamson song, "filling up and spilling over." With one more gasp, Mandy sank back against my upraised knees before sliding down so that she rested beside me.

She gathered me into her arms. In the heat of the closed and darkened stall, our bodies were slick with sweat. The straw crackled beneath us as we shifted.

"Damn, you're hot!" Mandy said as she kissed my neck and then my mouth.

"You too," I murmured in reply. If I was shocked at my own behavior, I wasn't about to acknowledge it.

I became aware of noises outside. The little pig was snuffling at the door. Footsteps in the grass and voices came and went right next to the stall. Reluctantly, I pulled away and sat up. I looked at my watch. I was already fifteen minutes late in meeting up with my sister and her family.

"Oh, God! I'm late," I said, scrambling into my clothes.

Mandy remained on the blanket, stretched out in all her naked glory. I felt my pulse quicken and fought the temptation to let my family just go home without me. I kissed her briefly and headed for the door.

"Don't you want my phone number?" she asked.

Chagrined, I stopped and looked at her. Of course I wanted it. She had a little frown on her face. I knelt down beside her.

"Mandy, I'm so sorry. I didn't mean to be so rude."

She smiled again and pulled a scrap of paper from her jeans pocket. Somehow finding a pen, she scribbled a number on the paper and handed it to me. She held tight to the paper as I went to take it.

"You *will* call me?"

"I promise."

"Don't forget your dog."

She grabbed my wrist and pulled me down for another deep kiss. I scrambled up, snatched the dog and left with one more backward glance. Her image burned itself into my memory. I knew I'd think of this moment for a long time to come.

I hurried to the place where I was supposed to meet the family. They all gave me impatient looks as I approached, especially my brother-in-law. My niece's eyes lit up when she spied my jumbo husky. She scurried over and held out her arms. I thrust the dog into them. It was almost as big as she was.

"You're all flushed," my sister scolded. "You were supposed to stay out of the sun. And you've got straw in your hair."

We headed through the gate and to the car. "Oh, I did stay out of the sun," I confirmed with a big grin. "I spent the last hour or so in the pot-bellied pig shed."

She looked at me.

"Guess it got a little too hot in there," I explained, thinking of Mandy as I fingered the scrap of paper in my pocket.

I fell silent, letting the memory wash over me. This was one trip to the fair I'd not soon forget.

Taboo

Tracey Richardson

Niki was lining up her pool shot, aiming for the
far corner pocket, when she heard that familiar but
distant laugh again. Curious, she looked up from the
velvety pool table, past the swaying couples on the
dance floor and found the table again.

Niki sucked in her breath, held it for a moment
as she eyed the shoulder-length wavy brown hair over
denimed shoulders, the infectious smile and those
cheekbones that belonged on a statue of an ancient
goddess somewhere.

"What are you looking at?" Niki's friend Mel

nudged her roughly. "We've got a pool game happenin' here."

Niki grinned, feeling that dazed, woozy sensation again. "I think I'll just burst if I don't ask her to dance, Mel."

"What the hell are you talking about?"

Niki pointed her out across the smoky bar, having not wanted to share her fantasy woman until now. "The sexy dark-haired one sitting with those other two women."

Mel shrugged broad shoulders. "Good-looking, if you dig older chicks. I'll bet she's close to forty."

Niki stared wistfully at the object of her simmering lust. The molten desire scorching its way through her was a welcome change from her three months of celibacy. "Who cares how old she is. I think she's hot. And anyway, I've decided to stay away from girls my own age."

Mel frowned. "Just because Maggie dumped you doesn't mean —"

Before Mel could finish, Niki had set her pool cue down and was brazenly heading toward the table of the three older women.

Niki wouldn't allow herself time to lose her nerve. She nodded, smiled at her fantasy woman and switched on all the charm a twenty-one-year-old butch could muster. "Hi. I was wondering if you would like to dance with me."

Mild surprise registered on the older woman's face, amusement flickering in her intense brown eyes. She looked quickly at her friends and must have found encouragement there. "Yeah, sure." Her smile was faint, her voice desolate of any emotion. Niki chose to ignore the uncertainty in the woman's demeanor.

Niki felt her knees weaken but replied with a smile she hoped was dazzling in its youthful exuberance. "I'm Niki, by the way," she said as she led the older woman to the dance floor. "What's your name?"

"Pamela."

Niki put her arms around Pamela's waist and held her closely, giving the older woman no choice but to put her arms around Niki's shoulders. "That's a gorgeous name. But then, I guess that's fitting."

Pamela looked up at her and tilted her head. "You're certainly not like any young woman I've ever met. Not that I've met many. I mean —" She faltered momentarily. "I don't usually dance with women I don't know. Especially women your age."

Niki grinned and pulled her closer, their faces just a breath apart. "Then how come you're dancing with me?"

Pamela's smile told Niki she had scored a point with her forthrightness. Her chocolate brown eyes bore deeply into Niki's. "I'm intrigued by your brazenness. Walking over to a table of strange women like you did and asking someone old enough to be your mother to dance takes real guts."

Niki laughed. "And I'm intrigued that you said yes."

They danced close, Niki inhaling Pamela's sweet, subtle perfume as her hands circled her back, stopping at the ridge of her lower back. Pamela's response was in her hands, which moved up to touch

the back of Niki's neck. It was all the encouragement
Niki needed as another slow song began.

She looked into Pamela's half-lidded eyes. "I want
to kiss you so badly."

There was no reply, just the tiniest challenge in
Pamela's smirk. In an instant, Niki's mouth was on
her, their lips melding. Niki gently tasted the supple
lips, her urgency hinting at more.

Pamela suddenly pulled back, but Niki's strong
grasp would not let her inch away any farther. "I'm
sorry, I —"

"No, no, it's me," Niki apologized, still holding
her tight. "I'm scaring you, aren't I?"

Pamela blinked. "It's just that —"

Niki boldly smothered her words with another
kiss, pressing hard this time, parting the soft lips
with her intensity. Her hands glided naughtily over
Pamela's tight round ass. There was no apology now,
just raw intention.

The kiss lingered until the song faded. Niki
pressed her cheek to Pamela's. "You're the sexiest
woman I've feasted my eyes on in a long time," Niki
whispered. "Come home with me tonight."

Pamela laughed and pulled away. "I don't think
so."

Niki grinned. "Then why don't we go back to
your place?"

"Definitely not."

Niki wasn't about to be dissuaded so quickly, but
she didn't have much time. The song had ended and
couples were separating. Pamela was glancing back at
her mates.

"Let me take you out for dinner," Niki offered.

Pamela hesitated, looking her young suitor up and down. Her agreement was in giving Niki her phone number. Niki grinned and responded by whipping out a pen and triumphantly scrawling the number on the palm of her hand.

They met at the restaurant, Niki chivalrously rising from her chair until Pamela sat down.

Niki practically drooled over Pamela, who looked smashing in a silky black off-shoulder dress that revealed tantalizing glimpses of both cleavage and thigh. Her skin looked so smooth, so enticing.

Niki breathed deeply. "You look wonderful." She lowered her voice to a whisper and winked provocatively. "I wish I could kiss you right now."

Pamela blushed, her eyes averted.

"Sorry," Niki apologized. "I'm being pushy again, aren't I?"

Pamela hesitated, fidgeting in her seat until a waiter came by and took their order for a bottle of Merlot and an appetizer of bruschetta.

"Niki," Pamela said slowly, her words heavy with that agonizing tone that implied rejection, or at least some sort of warning. Her fingers twirled the fringe of the table cloth. "I find your interest in me very flattering." She smiled generously. "I really do. You're so handsome and so sure of yourself. But . . ." She focused on her silverware, her smile dissolving. "I have a daughter your age. Margaret would just die if she knew."

"You mean because you're out with another woman?" Niki asked innocently.

Pamela shook her head. "No, no, she knows I'm gay. In fact, she's a lesbian herself."

Niki's eyebrows shot up. "Cool." She grinned.

Their wine and bruschetta arrived. Niki poured them each a glass.

"So, you were married once?" Niki asked.

Pamela took a sip of her wine. "Yes, a long time ago. Margaret's my only child. She's going into her second year at college." Pamela took another sip. "Are you a student?"

"Yes, I'm just about to start my third year in a pre-law program. I've been working as a gopher here this summer for a lawyer who's a family friend."

Pamela cocked her head. "You're not from around here, are you?"

Niki sipped her wine. "No, as a matter of fact." She coughed, feeling a stab of pain as she pictured Maggie. "A good friend of mine recommended this city, and the fact that my parents lined up a job for me was the deciding factor."

"Do you like it here?" Pamela smiled.

Niki grinned back, mischief sizzling inside her. "Better and better all the time."

They ate the bruschetta and drank more wine, but Niki felt unsettled by Pamela's seeming hesitation. She felt a desire for Pamela she hadn't felt in months, not since Maggie. But Maggie had ditched her for some college freshman, and now Niki was ready for something — someone — more serious.

"Pamela," she said softly, swirling the wine in her glass. "Why are you afraid of me?"

Pamela drew in a deep breath, her eyelids fluttering briefly. Her full lips trembled ever so slightly, a matching quiver in her fingers loosely cradling the glass of wine. Niki wondered what those soft, slender fingers would feel like on her, in her . . .

"I . . ." Pamela lifted her dark eyes to Niki's. "I'm sorry, Niki. I really wish I could be more . . . brave like you."

A small smile tugged at the corner of Niki's mouth. "What exactly are you afraid of?"

Pamela inhaled sharply. "The way you so obviously want me." She took a quick gulp of wine. "You're so young and desirable and . . ." She studied Niki's hands as Niki continued to rhythmically stroke her wineglass. Her eyes suddenly took on a smoky haze. "You could have anyone."

Niki grinned again. She felt like growling. "It's you I want, honey. And frankly, I don't care what your daughter would think of you out with someone her age."

Pamela smiled back, her shoulders noticeably relaxing, her eyes twinkling.

Just the permission she needed, Niki thought as she swept her fork onto the floor, where it skittered beneath the table. She pushed her chair back and crawled under the table, pretending to search for the fork. But she had other plans.

She felt a tickle low in her stomach at the sight of Pamela's trim but firm long legs covered in silky black hose. She couldn't seem to stop her hand, which worked in perfect synchronicity with her one-track mind. She trailed her palm up Pamela's calf and licked her lips as Pamela's legs parted slightly.

Her hand slid higher and higher up the stockinged leg, Niki's heart on fire now. God, she wanted this woman right here, right now.

With her free hand, Niki took Pamela's trembling hand and held it there in her lap. Her other hand glided up to Pamela's garter belt, stopped and caressed the inside of Pamela's thigh. Niki was breathing harder, the tickle in her gut having gone south, throbbing painfully. Her fingers migrated to Pamela's silk panties, and Niki heard Pamela gasp. Niki smiled and caressed the moistening panties, her fingers fluid and airy, as though she were playing a harp.

"Is everything all right, madam?"

Niki suppressed a giggle as she heard the waiter's voice. From the shelter of the tablecloth, she could see his shiny black shoes just inches away.

"Oh, ah, y-yes, fine," Pamela stuttered, sounding out of breath.

Niki slid the wet panties to one side, grasped Pamela's tight ass and pulled her into her mouth. A sharp gasp erupted from above. Pamela tried to squirm away, but Niki's firm hold wouldn't let her.

"Are you sure?" the waiter asked again. "Would you like to wait until your friend comes back before you order?"

Pamela must have nodded because the shiny black shoes disappeared. Niki closed her eyes and kissed the soft, juicy flesh, brushing her lips against Pamela's warm desire, wanting more. A kick from Pamela hit her squarely in the chest.

"Niki!" Pamela hissed. "We can't do this — not here."

Niki gave a final, commanding stroke with her tongue and pulled back, emerging from beneath the table with a silly grin on her slick face. "Then let's forget dinner and go back to your place."

Pamela glanced nervously around to see if anyone was watching them. She gathered up her purse.

Niki winked. "Your daughter's not there, I hope."

Pamela shook her head as she rose from her chair. "She didn't come home from school this summer." Her smile, for once, was wickedly indulgent. "Let's go."

Pamela had barely closed the door inside her two-story duplex before Niki pushed her up against the wall, her lips devouring Pamela's, her hands tightly holding Pamela's wrists at her sides. She kissed Pamela with a surprising fury, her mouth parting Pamela's lips, her tongue pushing its way in, jamming Pamela's throat. She wanted Pamela to take the length of her throbbing, pumping tongue deep into her mouth, her throat.

Pamela obliged, moaning, her eyes squeezed tight. Niki's right hand released Pamela's wrist and cupped a breast, then stroked the nipple through the silky dress. Pamela moaned again, and Niki trailed her lips, flicking her tongue, down her soft neck to Pamela's enticing cleavage. Her mouth nudged at the cloth, her teeth finally clamping it and pulling the dress down and over the swollen breasts. Niki's lips found an erect nipple, her tongue stroking it firmly as her hand moved to Pamela's thigh, pushing impatiently at the dress. Fingers found the garter belt, relieved a stocking and settled on the silk panties.

Pamela groaned. "Oh, God, Niki," she said between ragged breaths. You're . . . just . . . like I thought you'd be."

Niki beamed. Her mouth finding and conquering Pamela's other breast, she greedily pulled the panties to one side and thrust two fingers into Pamela's yielding wetness.

"No," Pamela breathed urgently. "Not here. Let's go up to my room."

Niki kissed Pamela's mouth again. "Anything you say, darling."

Niki playfully chased Pamela up the stairs, teasingly pinching her ass. Niki shed her jacket at the bedroom doorway, unbuttoned her shirt and kicked off her shoes. She kicked the door shut as Pamela lay back on the bed, rolling the stockings down her legs.

"Oh no, you don't." Niki laughed. "That's my job."

Niki leapt onto the bed, finishing the job of removing the stockings, then Pamela's soaked panties. She inhaled their scent, then tossed them aside.

"Oh, baby, you are so beautiful." Niki pushed the dress up around Pamela's waist, admiring what she saw before she delved right in, her mouth consuming Pamela, her tongue snaking its way into her.

Pamela abruptly pushed herself up onto her elbows. "I think I hear something, Niki," she whispered.

"It's only my beating heart you're hearing, honey," Niki answered, then resumed her mission.

Her tongue worked furiously, Pamela falling back onto the pillows again in pure capitulation. She moaned, breathing hard like she'd just run a marathon. Her hand clutched a fistful of Niki's hair as her hips gyrated to the rhythm of Niki's tongue. They rocked together in a synchronized dance of the most intimate kind, the bed creaking in time.

Without warning, the bedroom door flew open, the sound of it hitting the wall and reverberating throughout the room, crashing into Niki's and Pamela's private and very pleasurable world.

Pamela gasped sharply, pulling herself from Niki's mouth. A gasp from the doorway echoed in response.

"Margaret!" Pamela finally yelped, grabbing for a sheet or a blanket, or anything to cloak her obvious embarrassment. "What are you doing here?"

Niki turned then. The shock of what she saw stunned her, her throat clamping up like a vice grip. Her widened eyes felt like two giant orbs.

"Maggie!" Niki finally croaked, rolling onto her back with a groan. Her mouth felt as dry as chalk. "Aw, shit."

The Protest
Lisa Shapiro

I'm always careful with my placards. I take great care with my protest signs — neat block lettering, eye-catching color, slogan and layout — perhaps more so now that the money I earn has nothing to do with activism. In college my signs had a slapdash appeal. The underlying message — on the go and angry. Now, four years out of school and a graphic artist by trade, I'm out of practice but trying. The placard read, "Bad sports kill the game. Stop the hunt!" The letters filled the poster board in green, black and tan — camouflage colors — with the word *kill* in red.

I was taking such care with my sign because I was alone for another Friday night, an entire weekend, actually. Since Kimmie and I had parted ways, I hadn't dated. I'd done the party circuit but got the feeling that when I ducked out early our friends called Kimmie and said, "Come on over, girl. The coast is clear." Which summed up my social life in a word. Sympathy. Our friends were really her friends, and lately when they called I said, "No thanks." The breakup had been my idea. I'd given up a girlfriend, friends and social activities as though I'd gone to a car dealership and refused power steering, air conditioning and antilock brakes. My life had all the glamour of a stripped-down model. After a year of living together, I'd suggested to Kimmie that she get her own apartment.

She'd stared at me. "You want to split? Delilah and Shelly's wedding is this weekend."

"I'll go to the wedding, but I don't want to live together."

"You're breaking up with me?"

I could understand her disbelief. Kimmie did the dating, mating and breaking up. She'd approached me slowly, and that wasn't her style. She had lovers — hot and fast — and flew from dances to concerts to fund-raisers and art openings as quickly as ink dried on advertisements. I was the type to catch reruns. I'd been swept up in the courtship but soon found myself missing quiet nights alone. It seemed a natural step from saying, "You go tonight," to "Why don't you go?" Underneath the weeping, I sensed that Kimmie was relieved. She'd stayed longer than she wanted, than either of us wanted, because it had taken her so long to seduce me.

I sighed and held up my sign, the poster neatly stapled to a carrying post. Tomorrow when the sporting expo opened, featuring hunting and shooting gear, I'd be in top protest form. My social life was dead, but I had still had a social conscience. I propped the poster against my couch and went to bed.

In the morning I caught a bus downtown, wedging my sign upside down between my knees and the seat in front. At the expo center I was in place by the box office before the gates opened. A security guard steered me behind a safety line, closer to the exit than the entrance, where I joined a small but determined band of picketers — pro-animal, anti-gun. We clustered in a knot behind the cordoning ropes beside a trash can. By midmorning sportsmen and their families had formed a steady line at the gate. Vigilant, I hefted my poster. An hour later they began trickling out, munching popcorn and carrying fishing poles, sunhats and canoe paddles. Winter was edging toward spring, and as the show-goers marched past I could feel their excitement, bubbling like stream froth. Consumerism, I sneered. But the prospect of warm, sunny days tugged at me, too.

A few rough-and-ready types strolled by, and a man wearing a camouflage jacket exited bearing a crossbow. A cry erupted from our little gang. We yelled, "Shame. Shame." I shook my sign, but he barely glanced at us.

By noon my shoulders ached and I had to pee.

Clearly, I was out of practice. In college I'd done all the women's, civil and gay rights marches. Once, in a mile-long march on the statehouse, I'd borne a banner whipping against a headwind, then stood for hours listening to speeches without tiring. Here it was noon and I was tuckered. I weighed options. I could break at the Dunkin' Donuts and then return for the afternoon vigil. Or, and I had to admit that the second choice had more appeal, I could prop my sign in the trash can and get lunch. There was a Chinese place down the street. Lunch was winning. I hated to ditch my sign so soon, but if any of Kimmie's friends happened to call later, I could say in all sincerity that I'd had a busy day helping the anti-violence cause.

I was right next to the trash can when I glanced up and saw a woman who looked familiar. She was about my height, but with the compact build and confident gait of an athlete. My figure is more pear-shaped than I care for, especially now that I work plopped in front of a computer screen. I used to race from classes to the coffeehouse. I like to think of myself as private, intense, not staid. Had I really become so settled? I watched the dyke heading for the box office and racked my memory. Perhaps I'd glimpsed her from the fringes of a party, or in the women's bar. She wasn't from work. My office was full of sensitive heteros and one flashy gay man. But I couldn't shake the feeling that I'd seen her before — the wide eyes, full lips, dark hair trimmed back from a severe forehead. Her bearing almost crossed the line from confidence into haughtiness. I stepped closer to the cordon, bumping against the ropes in an effort to see. I ignored the glowering security guard and leaned over, forgetting to wave my sign, intent on getting a better look. She purchased a ticket. God — she was going inside. As she headed for the entrance doors her gaze swept my way. She saw me and smiled. Not a whole smile, just a quirk that brought the corners of her mouth up. Her dark eyes looked very bright. Shiny. She pushed inside.

I realized that my fingers hurt, and I slowly un-peeled them from my signpost. All thoughts of taking a break vanished as I hustled back to my station by the exit door. Time slowed. I stopped wasting thoughts on images of wounded wildlife, and focused my concentration in an effort to remember. How could I forget those eyes — so expressive. Not hard, as Kimmie's had been at the end, but inquisitive and bright, almost too bright, as though she were on the verge of laughter, or tears.

I blinked.

She blinked.

I'd been so lost in thought that I hadn't seen her come out, but she was standing on the other side of the safety rope. "Do I know you?" I blurted. "You look familiar."

"Don't you remember? We went canoeing last fall." All at once that awful weekend came crashing back. I'd gone along at Kimmie's insistence and then chickened out, stayed in the truck and drove to the takeout point with a muscular woman who so dis-dained my lack of guts that she pulled her ball cap over her eyes and refused to speak to me. After that, Kimmie stopped trying to cajole me into adventures. I'd been so engrossed in my terror of the whitewater

that I'd scarcely noticed another pair of dykes don-
ning life vests and maneuvering their craft into the
current.

"I'm Terry." She stuck out her hand. "And
you're —?"

I reached across the cordon. "Ann. The chicken
who never got in the canoe."

"Whitewater's not for everyone." She paused. "I
gave up on it too."

Our hands stayed connected a moment longer. In
her other hand she held a fishing pole with an
orange "paid" sticker on it. I asked, "What's that
for?" She looked at me quizzically. "I mean —" I felt
like a dolt. "What kind of fish do you catch?"

"This is a fly rod for trout."

"Oh." I didn't have a clue what that meant.

She said, "I need a new hobby. Carla and I split
up after that canoe trip. We fought the whole way
downriver."

"I knew it was over for Kimmie and me that
weekend too. We held on for a few more months, but
I quit trying." My casual admission stunned me. I
could still hear her angry cry. *You're giving up!*" I'd
given up trying to explain. How could I live with
someone I didn't consider a friend? I didn't like loud
parties or camping. God, was I really so boring? But
friendship wasn't about doing things, was it? When
Kimmie and I stopped dancing there was nothing to
talk about. After the music ended the uncomfortable
silence began.

"Well, that clinches it," Terry said. "If you want
to sink a relationship, go canoeing." She eyed my
sign. "You're not keen on fishing, are you?"

I glanced up. "I was protesting shooting sports. I didn't have anything else to do this weekend."

"Can you take a break? Would you like to get lunch?" Quickly, I wedged my sign into the trash can, turning it so that it faced toward people exiting the show. They could read it or not — I didn't have to stand around waving it like a flag. Then I hopped over the dividing ropes. We agreed on Chinese, but when we pushed through the doors at the restaurant, the place was packed. All the popcorn-munching families from the expo center had beaten us to the tables. "Takeout?" Terry suggested.

While we were waiting for our order, I used the ladies' room. In the tiny mirror above the sink, I looked the same as always — blonde hair caught back in a ponytail, hazel eyes staring straight ahead, lips not prone to smiling. People called me serious. Was it true? Was I immune to spontaneity? If I wrote a personal ad it would say, "Solemn blonde, not sure how to have a good time." That would set the phone ringing. I washed my hands and then rushed to the register where Terry was paying for our food.

She waved my wallet away. "My treat."

"Don't be silly."

"Never. According to my ex, I don't have a sense of humor."

I said, "I can't take a joke, either. Next time I'll buy."

Outside, she pointed up the street. "I'm parked over there."

"I rode the bus."

As we reached her car she said, "It's cold for a

picnic." True enough, a strong March wind had gusted up. "My apartment's close."

I was curious to see where she lived, and delighted when we got there to find great art, terrific art on the walls. I admired the paintings, recognizing a few by local artists, but I'd never seen any of the photos. As I circled the room I became convinced that I was seeing a unique, bold style. I asked, "Did you take these?"

"Yeah."

"You're good. Do you do it professionally?"

"It's a passionate sideline. Do you have any hobbies?"

"I like making friends. I used to be pretty good at it." I thought back to the days before Kimmie, to the people I used to know, the ones I could talk to. Maybe they were still around. Probably I should give them a call. Terry moved up beside me while I was studying one of her photo portraits. The woman in the picture had light hair and, in profile, a slight hook in her nose. She looked a little like me. "Is that your ex?"

"I don't know who she is. I saw her sitting in the park one day, and I snapped the shot."

"She looks pensive. What do you suppose she's thinking about?"

Terry said without hesitation, "Love. I've looked at that picture from every angle, and I think she's dreaming about a lover."

"Someone she's missing?"

"Or someone she hasn't found yet." She said it softly, and I turned to look at her. "She looks a little like you," she said. There was a long moment when neither of us spoke. I found myself enjoying the quiet, a silence that I felt no urge to break. My body was still, but I was full of a tingly, fluttery feeling that meant I was nervous, or excited. She asked, "What are you thinking about?" I didn't answer, just let our lips meet. She smiled. "Me, too."

Her hands went behind my head, and our bodies aligned. I didn't do this, I thought. Didn't meet a woman and kiss her. Not on a first date. I didn't date, just stayed home and reveled in solitude. I liked the weight of her hands on my shoulders, the pressure on my back, the tugging as she pulled my shirt free. "I don't —" My throat closed, strangling the rest of the sentence.

She met my eyes. "Don't want to?" Her fingers trembled on my spine.

My hands found their way under her shirt. My fingertips were inches from her breasts. "I'm no good at this." Not romance. I didn't make love — not since Kimmie, and not even with her during the last few months before our breakup. I was out of practice with friendship, too. I said, "I can't remember the last time I went to a movie. I haven't left the house in a month."

"There's nowhere I want to go." She smiled. "You have that pensive look, like the woman in the photo." She started to chuckle.

"What's so funny?"

"That I met you at the sports expo. I decided to try fishing because I was convinced I'd never date again." Her fingers swirled on my breasts. "Tell me what you're thinking about."

"Warmth." My head tipped back as she nibbled

my throat. "Closeness." I began lightly stroking her breasts.

"Close and warm." She sighed. "Those are my favorites." Our shirts came off. Between kisses she said, "I like a lover who thinks things through. Someone who knows her mind, but takes her time. I don't want to be with the most popular girl, or the funniest." She whispered, "I like to talk in bed, not over dinner."

I pushed my hips against her. "I can't tell jokes. I get too angry about politics, and then I forget to buy milk."

She unfastened my jeans. "So you go to protest marches, and make grocery lists." She met my thrusting hips with her fingers, and I cried out suddenly as the sweet flash popped like a camera bulb. She took my breasts into her mouth, first one, then the other, but she was laughing.

I hid my face in her neck. "How could anyone say you don't have a sense of humor?"

"Practically the only time I ever laugh is during sex." It was the funniest thing I'd ever heard, and I laughed out loud. I wanted to ravish her. Kneeling, I stripped off her jeans and then pulled her hips forward, guzzling, then slowing as she got wetter, letting her get the rhythm. I drank her, then caught her as she collapsed, tearful, into my arms. She was laughing and crying. "You're sweet."

"You're fun."

She got up, naked, and fetched the forgotten take-out, curling herself onto the couch. Half dressed, my jeans undone and my panties still damp, I joined her. We shared the food but didn't talk. It was an easy silence. When we'd finished eating, she moved into my arms and asked, "Do you have plans for tonight?"

"No."

"Tomorrow?"

"I'm free for the rest of the weekend." I skimmed a hand over her breasts. "How about you?"

She nodded to the fishing pole propped in the corner. "I was going to try to catch a trout."

My hand tightened around her breast. "Don't you dare." Words of protest welled up, arguments spilling one over another so that I was tongue-tied, hardly knowing which point to make first. *Depletion of natural resources, destruction of the ecosystem. Inhumane treatment of trout.* I opened my mouth.

She put her hands on either side of my head and kissed me. "You have that pensive look." She slid my jeans past my hips.

I jerked them off. "We have to talk."

She was laughing, and then I was, too, my protest abandoned.

Light and Shadow
Janet McClellan

Erin Donovan walked out of the grocery store hefting the two large bags in front of her and headed toward her dark blue extended-cab truck. The last two bags completed the orders for the part-time job she had created for herself. Two months ago she had managed to talk the owner of the grocery store into boosting his sales and doing a bit of community service. It had taken some wrangling to convince him that hiring her to deliver groceries to the homebound might benefit him financially. It did not hurt her case to anonymously contact the local newspaper to let them know about the proposed service. The grocer received so much free positive publicity that although suspecting the reporter's source, he quickly hired Erin.

The part-time job had been a necessity. It gave her pocket money and the freedom she needed to move unobtrusively through her new community. It also kept the curious at bay. A benefit of her new part-time job, Erin quickly discovered, was that as a delivery person she could garner as much information about a person as a priest or bartender. She learned how to pay attention to that information. Recently she had added a pharmacy to her entrepreneurial enterprise. The elderly, the lame, the bureaucratically tired and generally overworked of the community began to take advantage of the new service. Her income increased steadily.

She placed the grocery bags inside and secured the last of the ten deliveries she would make that day against the tailgate of the truck. It was the only delivery she was looking forward to. That final delivery meant she would have an opportunity to see Laura again. It would be her opportunity for business and emotional voyeuristic pleasure.

Three weeks earlier, the grocer had handed Erin the names and addresses of the homebound and their grocery needs. There had been an extra name. Laura Sandstrom. At first Erin did not think anything of it, although it seemed to ring a familiar chime. On the long drive into the county and up the winding tree-lined drive, Erin remembered where she had heard the name before. She recalled a recent article in the newspaper with a photograph of the woman displaying some pieces of pottery. Laura Sandstrom had received coverage for her original and unique pottery designs. Her works had begun to garner praise at a few Southwestern galleries and the homes of the wealthier local elite. The article hinted that Laura was a recluse. The newspaper's photographer had barely caught a vanishing left profile of the reluctant local celebrity.

On her first visit, Erin had waited patiently with the groceries at the front door after ringing the bell, wondering if the artist's reclusiveness was actually a case of full-blown agoraphobia. She did not have to wonder long. Erin heard Laura Sandstrom's voice over the outside intercom. Its warm, inquiring tones send a rush of interest through Erin's limbs. Laura asked for her patience and told her to wait until she got to the door from her workshop. During what seemed an terminable wait, Erin paced back and forth in growing aggravation until she heard the sounds of scraping and shuffling coming from around the west end of the house. Laura Sandstrom was laboriously making her way toward her. Supported by a walker, she carefully balanced her cast-enclosed foot and calf. A bicycle basket strapped to the front of the walker held a water bottle and notepad that jostled with every forward movement. It looked odd until Erin realized the walker afforded Laura the ability to carry items which would have been impossible with crutches.

Laura Sandstrom looked up from her halting labors and gave Erin a wry smile. "I'm not very good at this yet," she explained, standing near the corner of the house. "Why don't you follow me back to the kitchen door? I'd have to make five or six trips to get everything inside. I'll pay extra, if you like."

Erin's heart raced unexpectedly. Laura Sandstrom wasn't what she'd expected. "There's another house?" Erin asked, confused. The picture in the paper had been of such poor quality that she had expected a much older, weary and careworn woman. Laura Sandstrom was not a day over thirty. The light green sleeveless blouse and denim cutoffs revealed a light tan and sculptured, small sleek body.

"Not hardly. It's everything I can do to afford this. I was down in the shop when you rang. The intercom runs to all the outbuildings. I never thought about how convenient it was until I broke my foot. Now, it's a necessity," Laura said as she manipulated the walker to turn around. "Follow me. I promise I won't keep you too long from your rounds."

"No problem," Erin said and meant it.

Erin lifted the grocery bags and followed Laura back around the house to the kitchen door. While paying too much attention to the tight rounded shape of Laura's buttocks instead of to where she was walking, Erin almost tripped on a garden hose that was lying across the sidewalk. Refocusing her attention on her task, she stepped through the wide patio doorway off the kitchen and into the house. She set the groceries on a counter and watched Laura dig through her shorts pockets for money.

"You know," Erin began, "the next time you order, if you work in the shop a lot . . . I mean, rather than making you walk up to the front, I could just bring them around back here."

"That would work. It would save part of the walk," Laura said.

Erin smiled and looked out the patio doors across the sloping backyard and the deepening shade of trees. "Where is your shop?"

"Not as close as I'd like," Laura laughed. "Over there, she said, pointing. "Down that brick walkway and under those trees. The previous owners, an elderly couple, built a small greenhouse down there. It's heated, floored, cozy. I've put one kiln inside and another outside for use in the summer. I get all the nature and solitude I need. Perfect for my work but a bit awkward in my current condition."

"Will you have your cast on long?"

"Another six to eight weeks. Seems I did more damage to myself than I originally thought." Laura grimaced as she handed Erin the money for the groceries.

"There's an extra ten dollars here," Erin noted as she gave Laura the receipt.

"I know. It's my way of thanking you for going the extra mile."

"Well, I can't say I don't need it. Thanks."

"Don't let it get around. Most folks think I'm a churlish recluse. Eccentric and all that. Seems as though unusual reputations about personal habits are part of the art world." Laura's eyes twinkled as she spoke.

"I won't mention it to a soul," Erin said, shifting uncomfortably as she tried to keep her gaze averted. "I guess I'd better get going. Thanks again, Ms. Sandstrom."

"Laura. And thank you . . . ah . . . By the way, what is your name?"

"Erin. Erin Donovan. Let me know if you need anything else," Erin said as she walked out the kitchen door. Anything, she thought.

She made her deliveries to Laura as promised and began to look forward to the brief meetings. She began to save Laura's deliveries till last so she might prolong their encounters. Ringing the intercom, she would wait for Laura to struggle up the sloping walk from the tree-shaded, converted greenhouse. At those times, when the summer sun beat most ferociously, Erin noticed that Laura's efforts with the walker made sweat glisten on her skin. Sitting close together, Erin would struggle to pay attention to the nuances of conversation while her senses were ambushed by Laura's sweet scent, proximity and conversation. Erin felt her pulse race every time her hands brushed nonchalantly against Laura in close exchange. With the increasing directness of Laura's gaze, Erin was beginning to believe the interest was mutual. Erin became distracted from her obligations. There were moments when she didn't remember she had not filed an honest report or wonder about her duplicity. She was walking a dangerous line, and she knew it.

For three weeks Erin managed to keep her thoughts to herself but not the speculation of concern. She'd been going through the motions, steeling herself, determined to get the required photographs. Today was different. It had to be. She had a job to do, and all the fleeting palpitations of her heart had to be put aside.

As Erin made her Saturday rounds of deliveries,

she couldn't help but glance at the camera with its telephoto lens on the passenger's seat. She shook her head in consternation and set her lips firmly against her misgivings. She vowed that today she would take Laura's picture and fax the reports she'd been hired to provide.

In the driveway, she cut the engine and let it coast to a stop. Grasping the camera, she jogged down the hill and through the decorative brush. Fifty feet from the greenhouse she stationed herself near the low overhanging branches of a tree and raised the camera. A few seconds of focusing brought the sunlit interior of the greenhouse into sharp perspective. Her finger tensed and then relaxed. Moving the camera lens to search the interior of the greenhouse, she spotted Laura's walker near a long low bench. A light pink shirt and denim cutoffs had been tossed carelessly in the basket.

A movement to the right caught Erin's attention, and she shifted her aim. She saw Laura sitting below a revolving ceiling fan as she hunched over a slowly shaping image on the pottery wheel. Erin focused the lens on Laura. She watched her face, let the camera's eye travel down Laura's body, and felt her breath catch in her throat. A white, sweat-soaked muscle shirt, a pair of white bikini underwear and the foot cast were all that covered Laura. Erin's resolve faltered.

As if in a semi-trance, Laura focused intently on her work. Her face shifted from soft relaxation to frowning determination as she massaged the clay on the motor-driven wheel. The world beyond the focus of her concentration had seemed to have vanished for her. Suddenly she looked up, perplexity crossing her face, shrugged and went back to her work.

Laura's glance surprised and spooked Erin. She shook the feeling off, reasoning that it was impossible for Laura to have heard the distant soft whirring shutter advance of the camera's film.

The loathed task complete, Erin lowered the camera, shifted her position and cursed silently under her breath. In exasperation she dashed back around the trees and up the hill to her truck. She tossed the camera carelessly through the open window and walked stiffly toward the rear of the truck. She hefted the grocery bags and approached the house. Near the kitchen's sliding patio doors, Erin rang the intercom to announce her presence to the industrious Laura. She found a lounge chair, sat down and waited for Laura to hobble up the slope.

The following week, Erin was tardy getting to the grocery store. She had spent much of Friday night drinking, dancing and thinking. The fog that had settled over her mind had been washed into forgetfulness as she led a woman in her arms across the floor. When the bartender called for last rounds, Erin fancied the idea of taking the woman home. The idea vanished when Laura's image rolled through her mind. She politely and regretfully rejected her dance partner's advances and left. She's spent the weekend alone, drinking, unable to stop thinking about Laura.

Arriving late and hungover on Monday morning put every task behind schedule. It seemed to take forever to find all the groceries her customers had ordered, longer to get through the checkout and longer still to make her rounds. Dusk was falling on the summer night by the time she drove into Laura's driveway. Erin unloaded the bags, set them on the patio table and announced her presence over the intercom. Long minutes passed. Laura did not appear. Erin called again. There was still no response, and Erin's heart began to race.

Erin frowned in concern. It was unlike Laura not to answer. Erin looked anxiously toward the sloping hill where the greenhouse stood and headed toward it. As she rounded the bend in the walk, Erin could see the darkened greenhouse. She opened the door, found a light switch and flipped it on. Only the vacant potter's wheel greeted her.

Agitated and alarmed, Erin jogged back to the truck and found the snub-nosed .38 in the locked glove box. She pushed the revolver into the back of her jeans before returning to the kitchen patio. She tested the sliding glass doors and found they were unlocked. Swiftly and silently she entered the house. Her right hand rested on the butt of the revolver as she moved through the kitchen and into the interior of the house. The first floor was dark and empty. Near the stairway she bumped into Laura's walker. Its presence and Laura's absence sent a chill through her veins.

She drew the revolver and noiselessly took the steps up to the second floor. As she tiptoed down the long hallway, Erin noticed a light shining from under the bathroom door. She grasped the door handle, took a deep breath and burst into the room.

Laura screamed, and Erin returned it with her own startled yelp. To Erin's amazement, Laura was sitting in the tub, a damp towel half-covering her.

"Oh, Erin! Thank God you're here!" Laura gushed as she tried to sit up.

"What in the world?"

"I fell."

"You fell naked into the tub?"

"No, I was bathing. It's this damned cast. I'm supposed to keep it out of water. I had finished my bath, then I pulled the plug and tried to lift myself up. I didn't make it. I think I hit my head when I fell," Laura complained as she rubbed her head.

Erin put away the gun and went to Laura. "Do you think you broke anything else?" Erin looked at the awkward angle of Laura's soggy cast resting in the tub.

"Isn't the foot enough? No, I don't think so. I don't know. I passed out. Anyway, when I came to it was dark, my head was throbbing and I was still in the tub. Good thing I was letting the water out. I might have drowned. But more importantly right now, I'm freezing," Laura said as she shivered under the thin towel.

"Let's get you out of there. Put your arms around my neck and let me do the work. I don't want you to put any weight on that leg." Erin reached for Laura.

"Promise not to peek," Laura teased.

"Not on your life," Erin said as she lifted the lithe body from the tub. Erin balanced her on the tub's edge, shifted and lifted Laura up into her arms. "Don't worry about my looking. Think of it as my tip. One of those perks of the job." She hugged Laura to her a little more tightly than absolutely necessary. "Where's your room?"

"Is this how you operate? Wait until I'm naked and helpless, then simply carry me off to my room and your advances? Why, Ms. Grocery Person, where will this end?" Laura laughed, then cried out unexpectedly.

"What ... what did I do? Erin asked in alarm.

"Nothing. You didn't do anything. I wiggled the toes of my broken foot. I'm not going to do that again until I get another cast," Laura chided herself as Erin laid her on the bed.

Erin put a pillow under Laura's head, then headed into the bathroom. She emerged moments later with a box of Ace bandages and a pair of scissors. "Let's see if we can improvise on a cast. I should take you to the hospital, you know?"

"No, I can't. I don't want to. I'll be fine, really. I'll go tomorrow. I can wait."

"Maybe. But are you sure that's what you want to do?"

"Yes. Just stay with me. I promise I'll be fine. If it looks like I'm having trouble, you can take me then. Deal?"

Erin cut off the soaked cast. With sure and careful motions she laced the bandages and secured Laura's foot as best she could. "Your ankle still looks awfully black and blue. I hope it hasn't been injured any further. How's your head?"

"Fine. It's mostly my pride that's been injured."

"How do you mean?"

"Well, ever since you first brought groceries, I've been wondering what it would take to get you into my bedroom. I had no idea I'd make a complete fool of myself to do it."

Erin cleared her throat in surprise. "I don't mind rescuing fair damsels in distress, but you're right, there are easier ways," Erin said as she bent to kiss Laura. "Like, simply asking."

In a few moments they lay naked together in bed. Erin studiously avoided any moves that would endanger Laura's bandaged ankle.

Laura clung to Erin as Erin explored and caressed every delicious part of her body. Erin heard her name being called — reverentially, ardently, ecstatically — as she went down on Laura. Erin stayed with her as Laura's arousal soared, peaked and exploded time and time again.

Afterward Erin held Laura in her arms and reached for the tossed covers.

"I'd like to return the favor," Laura said dreamily.

"Not right now. You should rest. But don't sleep. I'm concerned about that bump to your head. It make me a little nervous."

"There's something that makes me a little nervous about you, too," Laura said apprehensively.

"Oh, and what would that be?" Erin pulled Laura closer.

"The gun. It's not the usual sort of thing for a delivery truck driver to carry, is it?"

"Now, you know even this town has a few rough neighborhoods," Erin responded evenly.

"Well, okay. Then, you did mention you used to live in a much larger city. I suppose there's that too. Or do you have visions of being an avenging Amazon?"

"Amazon probably, but avenging? I think not. Then again, maybe if you had been held hostage by bad guys instead of a treasonous bathtub, I could have rescued you then, too," Erin assured her and hoped she laughed convincingly.

"You seem awfully sure and confident for someone who seems satisfied to live in the middle of nowhere as a mobile grocery clerk. Are you hiding some mysterious past, Erin?"

"Oh, sure. Aren't we all?" Erin said softly as Laura turned in her arms and kissed her cheek.

"Well, mysterious or not. You certainly saved me in more than one way. Is there anything else I can do for you in the way of a reward?"

"I can think of a few things. But I would rather extract a promise that I can come over and see you with and without groceries in tow," Erin offered.

"That can be arranged," Laura said, and before Erin knew it, they were making love again.

Two days later Erin was sitting in her office listening to the brazen complaining voice of Lucinda Johnson as she screamed over the speakerphone. "I don't understand! I paid an outrageous retainer for your services. How the hell could you lose Laura Lyons after you finally located her? The people who told me you were the best don't seem to know shit! Let me make it simple. I want Lyons back, or whatever name she's hiding under now! I love her! And if you can't do the job I'll get someone who can."

"Trust me, I'll find her again. It's a matter of

personal and professional pride now," Erin spat back ferociously.

"Just see that you do. There won't be any twenty percent finder's fee if you don't, and I'll go to the state bureau and have your license revoked. Do you understand?"

"Perfectly," Erin said as she heard the phone slam down at the other end of the line. Erin closed her eyes and sighed heavily, remembering Laura's touch. Light and shadow, smoke and mirrors, Erin thought sadly. There was more to Laura than met the eye. Even knowing what she did about Laura Lyons, a.k.a. Laura Sandstrom, caused Erin to want her more. Her paying client could go to hell. This was a matter of pride. When she's returned to Laura's the day before, she found the studio and house cleared out. Laura had disappeared. Erin was shocked.

Erin flipped open the file folder and began to think about the thrill of the chase. It was personal, and Erin intended the final sweet capture and surrender of the elusive Ms. Lyons to be deeply personal and satisfying too.

Double Fantasy

Therese Szymanski and Barbara Johnson

Colleen glanced up as the elevator doors opened, then resumed reading the report her boss had given her to review. She'd only read three or four words when she looked up again to examine the back of the person who'd entered. Sure enough, her subconscious mind had registered the tall, leather-clad figure as a woman. She could feel her face flush as she noted the broad shoulders and slender but muscular body and the taut ass in its shiny black leather. The woman's body was tense, alert — like a panther ready to spring. Her dark wavy hair made Colleen's fingers itch to run through it. The short haircut exposed a neck shiny with the sheen of sweat. She remembered it was hot outside, but this woman still chose to wear leather. It made Colleen smile, and as the aroma of warm leather filled the confined space of the elevator, she suddenly felt that the pale blue linen suit she wore was too restricting. She had an unexpected urge to tear off her nylons.

The woman turned ever so slightly, and Colleen could see her strong profile. Her eyelashes were surprisingly long, and the full sensuous mouth curved up in a playful grin. It was as if she read Colleen's thoughts. Flustered, Colleen turned back to her report, her trembling hands making the papers rustle. The sound seemed to explode in the silence. Colleen felt her heart beating faster, and it was suddenly hard to breathe. The woman's cologne swirled around Colleen's nostrils. Colleen took a deep breath and, to her chagrin, dropped her entire stack of papers.

The woman turned swiftly, but Colleen was already crouched down and picking up papers. Two booted feet pointed at her, and then a pair of strong hands touched hers ever so softly as they helped gather up the papers. She took in another deep breath and looked up into a pair of the most intense green eyes she'd ever seen. There was something dangerous about them, but deliciously so.

"Thank . . . thank you," she stammered as she lowered her gaze and concentrated on her task. "It's so clumsy of me."

"No problem."

The voice sent shivers up Colleen's spine. She hurriedly finished gathering the papers, struggling to

ignore the burning sensation of the woman's hands
on hers. She stood, and the woman stood too. They
were very close together. Colleen was also tall, but
still shorter than the other by at least an inch or
two. The scent of leather and cologne intoxicated her.
She felt dizzy. Mesmerized, she felt compelled to look
into the woman's glittering eyes. As if hypnotized,
Colleen moved forward and closed her eyes, lifting
her mouth for a kiss. She felt the soft brush of lips
against hers when suddenly the elevator lurched to a
grinding halt, throwing her into the woman's arms as
the light flickered out . . .

The woman fell into Brett's arms as the elevator
jolted to a stop, her red-gold curls falling silkily
against Brett's cheek, her curvaceous body soft in
Brett's arms. Holding the woman tight, Brett leaned
back against the wall to steady them against the
sudden impact. The only sound was that of their
breathing in the dark stillness they found themselves
in.

"Maybe this trip wasn't such a waste," Brett said
just before the emergency generator kicked on to
bathe them in a dim, subtle light. She had rather
enjoyed being in the dark with the attractive woman.
She saw no reason to interrupt what had already
begun because of a mere mechanical problem; in fact,
she saw the sudden halt of the elevator as a damned
good reason to follow up on what the luscious
redhead had already started.

"What?" the woman asked, not moving from

Brett's arms. Her linen suit rubbed provocatively against Brett's well-oiled leathers, her perfume filling the air like an erotic dream, invading Brett's senses with its sweetness.

"Nothing," Brett replied, running her lips over soft locks of hair and dropping her hands down to cup the twin swells of the woman's ass. She was smooth and soft, just like Brett liked her women, and fit perfectly against her.

"Maybe we should do something," the woman said, pulling away slightly, apparently forgetting how freely she had been offering herself to Brett mere moments before, but her voice was low and throaty, as if she was already aroused.

"I am."

Brett pushed the woman against the wall, parting her thighs with her own leg and pressing her wrists to the wall as she brought her head down to again taste the sweet lips. Not many women fit against Brett's tall body like she did; in fact, only Allie had ever felt like this. But Allie wasn't here, and this sensuous woman, with her soft, silky legs, thick soft hair and tender lips, was.

"Oh." The woman gasped at the kiss, leaving her lips open for Brett, who first traced them, then entered them with her tongue, darting into her and staking her claim. The woman's mouth and tongue were warm and wet, and she willingly let Brett have her way, let her consume her mouth while she began to arch up against Brett's hard leg.

Brett dropped her hands down farther, pulling the skirt up to feel the sleek legs beneath. Brett caught her breath as she discovered the woman wore thigh-high stockings rather than pantyhose. Increasingly turned on, she brought her head down to kiss the pulsing hollow of her throat.

The sounds of their rapid breathing and the woman's low moans echoed in the small chamber, uninterrupted by the sounds of heavy machinery or pulleys. The moans were like ambrosia to Brett, encouraging her hands, lips, legs and body in what they were already doing.

Everything about this woman said she was young and naïve, but not so much so that she didn't already know that she liked women. Brett had felt her gaze from the moment she entered the elevator on the second floor on her way to a rendezvous on the tenth floor. Brett was supposed to meet a woman she had met the night before at a D.C. strip club while checking out dancers for her Detroit theater. But this would be a fine replacement for her, Brett thought as she again ran her hands down the skirt to touch nylon-clad legs.

"What's your name?" Brett asked, looking into wide, ice-blue eyes.

The woman's deep voice and the touch of her strong fingers on Colleen's thighs snapped Colleen out of the spell that had been cast over her. She felt the blush once more on her cheeks as she realized her skirt was bunched up around her hips. She wanted to look away from those bold green eyes, but couldn't.

"What's your name?" the woman asked again.

Colleen slipped from the woman's grasp and

smoothed down her skirt. She took a couple of deep breaths to calm her fast-beating heart. Her wrists tingled where the woman had held her firmly against the wall. She felt the ache between her legs, the wetness, the heat. Even her first encounter with Gillian hadn't aroused such an intense physical longing. Her whole body trembled with desire and, yes, even a little fear at the promise of what was to come that gleamed in the woman's catlike eyes.

"Colleen," she answered, horrified to hear her own whispered croak. "Colleen," she said again, more confidently.

The woman smiled and took Colleen's hand in her own. "Brett Higgins," she said as she kissed the top of Colleen's hand and then each fingertip.

Colleen felt the rush of heat through her body as Brett's lips touched her skin. She felt on fire, aware of the sweat that beaded up on her skin and dripped between her breasts. The warm air in the unmoving elevator seemed to tighten around her. She heard her own shallow breaths as the blood rushed to her cheeks once again. In the dim light, Brett's oiled leather glistened. Colleen watched as Brett slowly and deliberately took off her leather jacket, revealing a tight black T-shirt and strong, muscular arms. Brett grinned, her white teeth flashing.

"It's so . . . so hot . . . in here," Colleen said, backing away from Brett and those devilish eyes, almost tripping over the papers strewn on the floor.

"Yes, it is," said Brett, her low voice sending a thrill through Colleen. "Why don't you take off your jacket." A statement, not a question.

Breathless and confused, Colleen fought for reason. "Brett, I . . ."

With two quick steps, Brett approached her again and silenced her with a kiss. Her hands on Colleen's shoulders pulled off the jacket. Underneath she wore only a sleeveless silk blouse of deep royal blue. The jacket slithered off, and then Brett's fingers were firm against her bare arms. She crushed Colleen to her and kissed her again, her tongue thrusting demandingly into Colleen's unresisting mouth.

Colleen moaned deeply and helplessly as Brett first unzipped her skirt and then tugged it off. Somehow she had lost her shoes, but that didn't seem to matter now as Brett's muscular thigh pressed between her legs. She, in turn, pressed herself wantonly against Brett's hard body, her hands playing with the tight muscles of Brett's back.

"You want me to fuck you?" Brett whispered against her ear.

"I . . . oh, Brett," Colleen replied, her voice husky with arousal. Brett's hands were under the silk blouse, around her waist, running up to lace-clad breasts and down to the top of bikini underwear, her thumbs playing with the elastic. Her lips and tongue were hot against Colleen's neck, enjoying the salty sweetness of the woman's skin.

"I asked if you wanted me to fuck you," Brett said. Her thigh was hard against Colleen's crotch, again pushing her against the wall. Colleen could only moan her reply, her breathing heavy and labored.

"Oh, God, Brett," Colleen said with a moan, arching up against Brett's forceful leg. She reached down and guided Brett's hands up to cup the heavy fullness of her breasts, her nipples pushing against the lace of her bra. Brett felt down along the line of Colleen's thigh, starting at the hip and taking her panties down with her hands. She knelt to pull them off, with Colleen delicately raising first one foot, then the other, while Brett ran her tongue up the inside of her thighs above the stocking tops.

Brett roughly encircled each leg with her arms, then pushed Colleen's legs farther open. But just centimeters away from Colleen's soaked cunt, she tightened her grasp and picked Colleen up, forcing her legs up and around Brett's waist.

Colleen let out a loud gasp when her wet pussy landed firmly against Brett's belt buckle. Brett pushed her tighter against the wall, her mouth tugging at the hard pegs of Colleen's nipples through the smooth silk of her blouse.

She then pulled the blouse up and over Colleen's head and unclasped the bra. God, it was just so fucking hot to have a naked woman wrapped around her while she herself remained fully clothed. Brett loved the control and eroticism of it.

She ran her teeth over first one nipple, then the other, while her hands gripped Colleen's ass cheeks down low, pulling them lightly in opposite directions. She could feel the woman's wetness spreading, could feel how hot and turned on she was.

Colleen squirmed in place, then pulled Brett's

muscle shirt out of her pants, reaching beneath the cotton to her skin, until she finally grabbed the shirt and pulled it up and over Brett's head. Brett wore no bra, leaving her chest bare and touching Colleen's own nakedness.

"You wanna get fucked, don't you?" Brett growled, holding Colleen tight as she reached for Colleen's soaked cunt. She let her fingers pause briefly to part Colleen's lips before barely tracing the outline of that wet pussy.

"Oh, God, yes," Colleen breathed.

"Then say it," Brett ordered, yanking down her zipper and the front of her boxer shorts, pulling out the long fat dildo she was packing.

"I . . . I can't," Colleen protested.

"Say it!"

"Fuck me, Brett. Fuck me! Please!" Colleen groaned.

Brett's fingers were already running a line up and down Colleen's clit, drawing her wetness across the swollen flesh and tracing a circle around her vagina.

"I want you inside me."

Brett thrust first one finger, then another, into Colleen, enjoying the slick tightness, before she withdrew them to guide the head of her dildo into her. She slowly released her hold on Colleen just enough so that she still rode the thick instrument.

Colleen gasped as it entered her, slowly filling her up. "Oh, dear God!" she cried out.

Somewhere in her mind, a warning whispered

softly. Her vulnerability was totally exposed. Not only was she in a public place, but a stranger — albeit an extremely attractive one — was doing things to her that she hadn't imagined in her wildest fantasies. Stop this, her inner voice said, but she ignored it, wanting only to feel the excitement of being completely filled, completely taken. Gillian flashed briefly into her thoughts, only to be replaced by pure pounding sensation as Brett plunged deeply into her very core. Against the elevator wall, her body moved in rhythm to Brett's thrusts.

The steel wall was cool against her hot skin. Brett held her firmly. Holding tight to Brett's strong arms and shoulders for support, she could feel Brett's muscles trembling. She could hardly breathe, especially when Brett's teeth against her neck made her gasp with pain.

"You're so tight and wet," Brett groaned into her ear. "C'mon, baby, ride me good."

"Brett," Colleen said, her voice breaking. She bit hard into Brett's shoulder to keep from screaming.

Brett moaned again and pushed into her, fucking her hard. Her fingers bit into Colleen's ass. The heat in the confined space barely matched the heat of their bodies. Brett was naked from the waist up. Their breasts melded together and then apart as their slippery, sweaty bodies slid against each other.

Colleen locked her ankles together, feeling the muscles of her own legs weaken and tremble as she struggled to hold on to Brett. She opened her eyes briefly. Brett's head was thrown back, her eyes tightly closed, the shadows from her long lashes fanned across her cheekbones. She breathed deeply from her open mouth. She thrust once more into Colleen and opened her eyes, their green depths boring into her, impaling her as she herself was being impaled.

"Brett, I . . . I can't . . ." Colleen implored as she felt the strength draining from her.

Brett pulled away and gently lowered her to the floor. Kneeling above, she leaned down for a kiss. Colleen grabbed her head and thrust her tongue deep into Brett's mouth. She ran her hands over Brett's shoulders, across her collarbone, and then squeezed her breasts.

"So, you haven't had enough," Brett murmured with laughter in her voice.

Her hands and tongue traced a path down Colleen's quivering body. Colleen involuntarily spread her legs, arching up against Brett's mouth as it moved across her belly and lower still. When hot mouth met hot pussy, Colleen felt like she could explode. And when Brett's long fingers finally thrust deeply into her, she did, screaming out Brett's name.

Brett licked and sucked and thrust as Colleen came to a tremulous release. Drained completely, Colleen could only lie limply. Her body tingled everywhere that Brett had touched. When Brett moved and knelt beside her, smiling down with a cocky grin and laughing eyes, Colleen could feel her whole body flush beneath that intense gaze. In the dim light, Brett's skin glowed — no, sparkled — with beads of sweat. Colleen placed her hand on one leather-clad thigh, her skin white against the black. The heat from Brett's body radiated through, making the leather feel soft and supple. She blushed again furiously as she caught sight of the dildo still peeking from Brett's pants. Laughing, Brett put it inside her pants and zipped them up. The sound echoed in the silence.

It is so damn hot in here, Colleen thought as she said aloud, "I've never met anyone like you," and instantly felt foolish and very naïve.

"We've got everything under control now," a male voice boomed over the elevator's loudspeaker.

Suddenly, the lights flickered back on and the elevator motors hummed to life. The woman pulled out of Brett's arms, her breathing heavy and her movements unnaturally slow. Her ice-blue eyes looked into Brett's.

Surprised to find the woman fully clothed, Brett shook her head slowly. Something very strange had just happened, and even thinking back on it sent a chill down Brett's spine, causing her to shiver. She slowly licked her lips. "Have we met somewhere before?" she asked.

The woman stood perfectly still. "I don't think so." Her arms hung loosely at her sides. The elevator stopped with a ding, and she glanced up at the floor marker. Fifth floor.

"Is this where you get off?" Brett asked with a grin as she quickly picked up the spilled papers and handed them to her.

"Yes," the woman said, taking the papers. "Yes, it is." She stepped off the elevator, then suddenly turned back toward Brett, nearly bumping into her.

Brett steadied her. "Did you forget something?"

"No . . . yes . . . I mean no." She turned and hastened down the hall.

Brett glanced at her watch. She really didn't have any time to spare before her meeting with that cute number on the tenth floor, especially with the elevator delay. Holding the elevator door open, she watched the curvaceous figure hurrying down the hall away from her. "Aw, what the hell," she said, and followed.

After all, sometimes fantasies do come true.

Colleen heard the elevator doors close, and then the sound of muffled footsteps in the carpeted hall behind her. She gave a quick backward glance. The darkly handsome butch in leather followed. With a tremor coursing through her body at some fleeting memory, Colleen smiled and slowed her step.

Sheila

Penny Hayes

You know, Sheila, nine years after the fact, I still could be resting on the top of a mountain I'd struggled throughout the day to climb or be standing behind my desk before my most rambunctious, seventh-grade students or be happily walking down the street, and it would happen. Someone would pass by, either known to me or a complete stranger, and something about that person, the color of her hair, a flip of a hand, some tiny little thing, would trigger remembrances of you that were so strong that my heart would lunge painfully, and I would have to grab a fragment of rock from the mountaintop, crushing the piece into my palm, or clutch the edge of my desk until my hands hurt, just to keep myself anchored to reality.

You were so tall and tan in the summer sun wearing that muscle shirt and cutoffs that day I first met you. Your eyes so big and blue that I was drawn to them as though they were gigantic magnets. Meeting at that backpacking school was such a stroke of luck for me, where, after a week of hiking, you called it quits because your heels were so badly blistered that you couldn't go on. I was more than willing to hike out to the nearest trailhead with you where you would be picked up and taken back to the main camp. But it was impossible for me to let you go like that, to watch you get into the van that would return you to your car and therefore take you out of my life forever. You could so easily disappear, and I just couldn't have that happen. So I told the trail master I wouldn't be going on and talked you into driving as far as my house for the night, a hundred miles away.

You parked in my driveway with another three hundred miles ahead of you tomorrow. But I could see you didn't want to leave. Then it got dark, and I couldn't do anything but invite you to sleep beside me. That's all that was supposed to have happened, but it didn't. You were on top of me, I was on top of you, our fingers roaming over each other's skin. You were so passionate, your kisses all over my face, your hands like hot irons running up and down the insides of my thighs — and more. I couldn't let you go; I had to have you, had to run my fingers through your long, glossy, tan hair, feel your teeth biting my shoulder, hear your breath as your tongue tickled my ear. You draped your long legs over mine while I lay the length of you, stroking your tongue with my own. I shall not ever, ever, ever forget how compelling your voice sounded when you came, as your arms grasped me with the strength of steel bands, holding me as though there would never be another time — and, as it turned out, there wasn't.

I still ache with your going, but I would never again put myself in that vulnerable a position, not if my very life depended on it, because to this day, to this minute, I still feel a terrible sense of loss. I have been so lonely without you all these years. So now that you've suddenly and unexpectedly dropped into my life, Sheila, *don't do it again*!

Tattered Pages

Marianne K. Martin

Lil contemplated the old black-and-white photos, committing to memory each place and expression she saw there, remembering a laugh, or a kiss, or a special place. Her fingers, missionary pale from too much time indoors, carefully turned each page by its tattered corner.

It was time she put an end to it — to the scrapbook first, and watch the flames of her evening fire erase thirty-five years of memories only she could know and then to the crumbling old temple of her body. Once rod-straight atop a champion show horse, her back now ached in its fixed, osteoporotic bow. The shapely jodhper-clad legs gripping tightly to the sides of the horse in the pictures, now shuffled slowly between the metal pods of the walker. Her eyes, although still a magnetic blue, she thought with pride, stared blurrily at a world she was too old and too tired to make a place in anymore. All the precious parts of her seventy-six years were gone. There was nothing left that was important to her, and nothing left that was important to anyone else.

Doc Hatcher had made it easy, whether knowingly or not, refilling her prescription for the third time without question. And Lil had done her homework; her stockpile was sufficient enough to slow her heart and respiration rates to a state of comatose within thirty minutes and, barring intervention, eventually still them completely. She knew exactly how many it would take, lined up neatly beside the old blue Fiesta glass. It would be over in a dignified sleep, her favorite hand-knitted shawl wrapping her shoulders as she nestled comfortably between the wings of her reading chair.

The flames of the fire would burn the last of the small logs, cut and stacked dutifully each week by the kindly young man down the road, and she would listen to its crackling accompaniment while she read for the last time the words of her beloved Vince. They would be the last thing in her heart, the first thing spoken when they were finally face to face once again.

She turned the final page of her scrapbook. Her fingers lingered lovingly over the handsome face and the laughing eyes that had loved her all these years.

What she would give to touch his face once again. She imagined the warm flush of it beneath the gentle caress of her hand and repeated the words: "Remember, we'll be together, always and forever." Vince hadn't just said the words, they both believed them. Death could keep them apart only so long. Ten years was long enough. It was time. Soon they would be new again — where they would ride and dance, and their hearts would soar again in love.

Lil closed the back cover, then opened the book at its beginning for one last look. With resolution she reached for the glass, then sat forward with a start at the knocking on the old farmhouse door. Past nightfall on a Monday there should be no callers. She thought to let the visitor knock in vain, but realized that if they knew her, they knew she would be home. She couldn't chance their persistence intervening before the pills could do their work. The intruder would have to be graciously excused and sent on their way. Deliberately she made her way across the room to the door where the visitor waited between knocks.

A young woman smiled shyly through the screen door. "Aunt Lil, do you remember me? I'm Elizabeth, Margaret's next to youngest."

"Oh, my," she said, surprised. "You're all grown up. Here, come in. Come in. Where's my hospitality?" With a smile and a gesture of her hand, she indicated that they should visit on the sofa. "What in the world are you doing at this old woman's house?"

"Hoping you'll forgive my waiting so long to come on my own. I've wanted to see you for a very long time."

Large eyes, nearly as blue as her own, stared their innocence into Lil's eyes. "There's nothing at all to forgive. You were just a little thing — too young to understand the disagreements of adults."

"I still don't. You and Uncle Vince were always so good to us kids. All week long all we could talk about was coming here on the weekend. Riding the horses, pickin' beans, splittin' wood — we loved every minute we spent here. When I got older I thought our parents were jealous that we wanted to be here so much."

"No, it wasn't jealousy . . . just something that couldn't be helped."

"After Uncle Vince's heart attack. Dad said having kids around would be too much for his heart. But we wanted so badly to see you both that the four of us spent hours making a list of things we would do to help you, and promises of how careful we would be around him if they would let us visit."

Tears filled the old woman's eyes. "You sweet, sweet children. I think of all we must have missed. I can see your little faces still."

"Not so little now. Danny's six-two now and has his own contracting company. He'll be married in April. Denise was married two years ago and stays at home with their little girl. Lisa is in her first year at Western on a track scholarship. I graduated last year from Miami of Ohio with a degree in music education."

"And your folks? How are they?"

"Lisa says they're fine. Dad was diagnosed with diabetes, but I guess he has it in check. I haven't seen them myself in five years."

"Dear girl, why not?" Lil frowned in concern.

"We had a disagreement of sorts too." She glanced up at Lil. "I've been okay. I didn't need their help. I worked three jobs, spread my classes out over the summers and put myself through. And I have a lot of friends."

"But they don't take the place of family, do they? There's a hole in your heart," she said, enveloping Elizabeth's hand in the warmth of her own. "That's why you're here."

Close enough, Elizabeth thought. She hadn't seriously considered telling her, had she? A woman known only through the eyes and heart of her childhood. Merely the thought of walking in after all these years and confessing that she was a lesbian was totally unreasonable. Lil may not even know what the word meant. What would they have called lesbians fifty years ago?

Lil squeezed her hand and patted the back of it reassuringly. "You get comfortable here by the fire. I'll get us something to drink."

"Can I help you?" Elizabeth offered, watching her great-aunt rise painfully to the walker.

"No, no. These may not be the legs of a champion horse, but there's still a touch of hospitable pride in this old heart. Once I get going, I don't always need this humility wagon," she said, plopping the metal legs of the walker down firmly before her.

Elizabeth picked up the photo album lying on the table next to the wing chair. *Why do we have to get old? Why can't we just move on the our next mission, in the next realm, if there is another realm, and put our lifetime's worth of strength and confidence and knowledge and abilities to a higher challenge?* She looked at the photos of a once vital young woman laughing with her sisters, hiking in the Grand Canyon, gliding effortlessly with her horse over a jump. Either old age or disease will take it all, everything that makes a person who she is, everything that makes life worth living, and take it in such a degrading manner. There had to be a higher plane of intelligence that she hadn't reached yet, that would allow her to understand the logic of it. She turned carefully the tattered pages of Lil's life. Maybe in this higher plane family wouldn't turn their backs on family. Instead, maybe they'd love and understand one another — share each other's joys — lift each other up from sorrow. Surely they would not allow an old woman to bear her husband's illness and death alone.

Vince's smiling face stared at her from the page. A gentle-hearted soul, he held a wide-eyed little Danny up to touch the horse's velvety nose. What disagreement could have torn a family apart for so many years? What couldn't be forgiven, even for the sake of attending his funeral? She wondered if it would be the same if *she* were to die tomorrow, leaving the mourning to friends and ex-lovers, her remains buried next to strangers. What a cruel joke love was. Where had she gotten the idea that it was a bond so tight that virtually nothing could break it? Books? Movies? There were no living examples that she could think of. Her parents were always only one more argument away from divorce, living together only because it was financially easier. They continued to fight over everything, except the abomination of homosexuality. At the normally idealistic age of twenty-two, she already had an automatic suspicion of all relationships. Lovers would always come and go, her brother would marry and cheat and divorce, her sister would put up with her husband's demanding ways for the sake of their child, and Lisa would eventually have her romantic heart broken — probably more than once. It was life as she knew it.

Elizabeth turned another page and realized Lil must have been looking at the album when she arrived. She wondered when mourning had ended and reminiscence began. *How long would anyone mourn over the likes of Elizabeth Justin?* As she turned the final page, a yellowed piece of newspaper slipped from behind the last photo. She pulled it the rest of the way out and read:

THE GAZETTE   May 3, 1986

LIFE OR DEATH ENDS 30-YEAR CHARADE

Emergency personnel, responding to a call late Thursday night, were shocked to find that what they thought was a male heart-attack victim was in fact a woman.

In a frantic call, Lillian Patterson stated that her husband, 64-year-old Vincent, was having difficulty breathing and was turning blue. The truth was discovered en route to the hospital when the victim's heart stopped.

The discovery ends a 30-year charade that started when the couple began dating. They were married in a church ceremony in 1963 before unsuspecting friends and family. Lillian Patterson (Justin) admits she was fully aware that she was marrying a woman.

Vincent (born Venessa) Patterson is in stable-but-serious condition at St. Andrew's Hospital.

At the shuffling sound of her aunt's footsteps, Elizabeth quickly tucked the article behind the photo. Unbelievable, she thought. All those years when no one knew. And then the years that they did. What must she have suffered? What must she be suffering still?

Then came the realization. Elizabeth rose quickly, took the drinks from her aunt's hands and placed them on the table. She cradled Lil's arm for support and embraced her. With a kiss to the softly wrinkled cheek, she said, "I think you have a lot to tell me" — she smiled — "about love."

Imagine

Therese Szymanski

It was gonna be another one of those nights, Jennifer just knew it.

The double bourbon she had before leaving her house did nothing to fortify her, to give her the beginnings of the transformation she'd have to make to get through the night. Even listening to loud Prince music in the car as she headed toward downtown Detroit did nothing to help transport her out of her own body and into that alter-ego she relied on.

She hadn't really felt like even coming into work,

which wasn't surprising in the least, because some of her coworkers were true bitches. Regardless, she told herself when she parked her car, tonight was a Friday, and she couldn't afford not to work on one of the busiest nights of the week.

She entered the building from the back and quickly moved over the dirty floor, layered with discarded condoms, dirty underwear and old makeup, and went to her locker. She threw her bag on a nearby chair, undid the lock and took a deep breath. She pulled her baggy old sweatshirt up over her head, took off her simple cotton bra, unbuttoned her jeans and stepped out of her underwear.

On went the tiny black g-string, fishnet stockings with a seam running up the back of one leg, black spiked heels, a black leather bra and tight black leather skirt. She deftly applied mascara and eyeliner, red lipstick and blush. A few touches of the curling iron to her long blonde hair, and she was done.

She looked herself up and down in the mirror, gracefully tossing the long locks over her shoulder before releasing a slow, seductive smile. The blue eyes were no longer Jennifer's, and it definitely wasn't Jennifer she saw in the mirror; Jennifer was gone, replaced instead by *Imagine*.

She walked to the door leading to the bar and waited. Steve, one of the bartenders, greeted her with a sleazy smile before bringing her a double shot of whiskey, which she downed in a single gulp while she let the loud music flow over her, possessing her with its beat. Its pulse became her pulse, pounding through her veins and arteries, sending blood down to her cunt, making her gyrate her hips to its rhythm.

She turned to Steve, slowly taking him in with her best bedroom-eyed gaze, while a knowing grin danced over her lips. He brought her another drink, which she downed in the same economic manner as the last, and then wrapped her arms around his thick shoulders, drawing him in close to her. He pushed his pelvis against her, letting her know he was ready when she was. She ran her lips over his ear, trying not to notice the hair there.

"Imagine, why don't we go in the back?" he whispered.

"This one's name says it all," a sleazy voice bellowed over the speaker. "Just let Imagine take you there!"

"Maybe later," she whispered to Steve, knowing damned well that later would never come, then turned and sashayed onto the small stage.

Exposé and Star were already onstage, dancing around wearing only their heels and g-strings, the flashing, colored lights dancing over skin that was already wet with sweat. Exposé's dark black skin contrasted against the near-alabaster of Star's untanned limbs and full white breasts.

Imagine was briefly transported back to a night a few months ago. The bar had closed for the evening and the three of them went to change back into themselves. Imagine had already discarded her g-string when she felt a hard stare against her back. She turned and caught Star slowly licking her beautifully full red lips, her hand slowly moving in her own pussy while she leaned back against a table.

"Do you ever get so turned on out there, being so exposed in front of so many people, that you almost can't stand it?" Star had asked her then, her voice deep and husky. Imagine then felt Exposé's naked body against her back, saw the gentle black hands caressing her body, exploring her swollen, shaved clit, teasing her suddenly taut nipples. Watching, Star smiled.

Imagine knew she was wet when she knelt in front of Star to taste her, to let her tongue roam in Star's depths. She had spread her legs when she knelt, inviting Exposé to lie between them, to taste her own sweetness while she lapped up Star, running her tongue over the swollen lips, dipping her fingers into her warm, slick interior.

Just thinking about it now made Imagine want to reach down to touch herself as she looked at the beautiful near-naked bodies in front of her. She took a breath to pull herself back into the present.

The smoke in the bar was thicker than usual, and Imagine tried not to notice all the men in the audience, smoking their cigarettes and fat cigars. She tried to let Imagine, with her cocky sexuality, flow through her, over her, while letting the alcohol gently impart its warmth and numbness on her.

She strode to the center of the stage, moving her hips and glancing over the audience with a sultry, unseeing gaze. She spun around and suddenly Star was pressed up against her, her leg between Imagine's, her naked breasts with their hardened nipples pressed against her own, her hands wandering over Imagine's body, taking liberties by running them over her ass, up her legs and under her skirt.

She felt Exposé against her back so that she was
sandwiched between the two women. She leaned back
against Exposé and hooked her fingers into Exposé's
tiny g-string. Star reached around Imagine and
grabbed Exposeé's ass, while Exposé's hands cupped
Imagine's breasts, slowly working around to undo the
top so she could squeeze the already hardened nipples
while Star unzipped her skirt and tossed it aside.

The men yelled their appreciation, and Star dropped to her knees so her breath was hot on Imagine's
already soaked clit. Imagine reluctantly cupped Star's
head and brought her back to her feet. Exposé left
her and went out to start the lap dances.

Star and Imagine gradually broke away from each
other, each to dance alone on the stage and allow the
men to slide tips into their g-strings. As each tip was
deposited, Imagine allowed brief dalliances — a hand
on her leg, a face between her breasts, a cupping of
her ass.

Star moved out into the audience, and another
dancer joined Imagine on stage. Imagine noticed a
guy walking up to the bar to get a drink before
going to his table at the back. She had never before
seen him in here.

He was slender and rather short, probably only
about five-four, and was attired better than most of
the other patrons in a neat double-breasted blazer,
slacks, and a tie that was still fully tightened.

Imagine could see that he was already turned on,
and it was a monster. She wanted to look away from
him, disgusted, but couldn't, even though she usually
didn't notice when a new guy came in.

He sported a very thick five o'clock shadow, as if

he thought the Don Johnson look was still in style, and his short black hair lay brushed back over his ears. His dark eyes met hers across the smoky room just before he sat down, adjusting himself along the way, she noted with disgust.

When she left the stage to begin the lap dances, she stopped by the bar to allow Steve to quickly refortify her. She didn't look at the man in the corner, because she was afraid he'd want a dance. Instead, she worked her way around the bar, moving to the music in the laps and arms of first one, then another and another, swaying just inches away from their hardened dicks while they lay their hands on her thighs, trying to move up to her tits, which were just centimeters away from their faces, their mouths.

The night passed in a blur with her trying to avoid those haunting dark eyes. Finally, she found herself doing a dance at the table next to his. She glanced over at him while she rode a customer's lap with his hands on her thighs, moving up her waist. Because of the smoke and darkness of the bar, she couldn't quite see his face clearly, but she could make out certain things about him.

He watched with a smirk on his fine features, his skin amazingly smooth. She couldn't tell if he was twelve or forty — he seemed ageless. His face and skin appeared young, but those dark eyes held secrets and truths she couldn't even guess at. She was drawn to him even while she avoided him. He both repulsed and intrigued her.

That night she dreamed of him. She was in her living room, on the couch with someone she knew only as a very attractive woman. The woman's soft hands were on her body, and Jennifer was leaning forward to kiss her when she became aware of another presence in the room. She turned and saw the guy from the bar, but he was standing back in the shadows so she was still unable to see him clearly. She spread her thighs, wanting the woman to take her under his watchful eyes.

The rest of the week Jennifer found herself longing to see him again, but come Thursday he still had not reappeared.

Friday afternoon she had lunch with her best friend, Lynn. Almost against her will, she found herself ranting and raving to her about this strange fellow.

Her green eyes blazing, Lynn looked across the table at her. "I'll tell you what I keep telling you — you need to move back in with your folks until you finish school. That way you'll be able to quit dancing and you won't have problems like this."

"We both know I can't do that. I'd still have to cover tuition, and I'd never be able to get any studying done with all those kids running around the house." Jennifer was the oldest of six children. "My parents can't afford to help me through school."

"I don't like the idea of you dancing." Lynn leaned across the table and took Jennifer's hands in her own. "I keep worrying that some day Imagine's just gonna move in and kick Jennifer out, and I don't want to lose my best friend."

"You know that's never gonna happen," Jennifer replied with a laugh. "It's just that this is the easiest way for me to make money right now. I make more in a night then a lot of students do in a week of working for McDonald's."

"I just wish I could get into that damned bar of yours to keep an eye on you." Lynn had previously tried to watch Jennifer work, but she couldn't get into the bar unless she was escorted by a man.

"Don't worry about me, hon. I've never dated men before, and I certainly don't intend to start now."

"You'd better not, 'cause there'd be a lot of awfully disappointed lesbians out there."

"Yeah, but that still doesn't stop them from taking off running when they learn what I do for a living." Most of Jennifer's relationships had been rather short-term because the women she liked couldn't live with the fact that she was an erotic dancer — she wasn't quite sure if it was jealousy or fear or what that caused them to take off, but all she knew was that she hadn't gotten laid in quite a while, and that just might be the reason this weird guy kept sticking out in her mind.

She got home that night, threw a carefully selected costume into her bag and headed toward the bar.

En route she thought of those fine features, those long fingers that she had seen light a cigarette the weekend before. She imagined those fingers running up her legs, caressing the insides of her thighs, hooking into her g-string. She felt the full lips against her collarbone, making their way over her exposed skin to the tops of her breasts.

Even in the heat of the car she felt her nipples tense and extend under her cotton bra, against the thick sweatshirt she wore to guard against Michigan's cruel winters. Unconsciously she parted her legs a bit, raising her crotch up toward the steering wheel.

He would be a gentle lover, unconscious of his own needs, wanting only her to satisfy him. Almost feminine, butch, in the way he made love to her, in the way he fucked her.

She arrived at the bar early to quickly survey the crowd before her transformation. Her palms were sweaty, so she ordered a drink to keep her company while she changed.

"Hey, baby," Star said when she entered.

"How's it goin'?" Jennifer asked, carefully putting on her makeup.

"Oh, it's okay," Star's voice was muffled as she pulled her sweater up over her head. "Hey, that weirdo guy from last week, the one who couldn't keep his eyes off you?"

"Yeah?" Jennifer said, whipping around to face Star.

Star appeared startled. She stopped changing, wearing only her slinky bikini underwear, and cocked her head at Jennifer. "Hold on, I didn't think you were interested in the boys."

Jennifer stopped. "I'm not. I just noticed him last Friday is all."

Star walked up to her and wrapped her arms around her. "Are you sure about that?" she panted into her ear. Jennifer was all too aware of the firm, pert breasts with their hard nipples pressed up against her. She felt Star's thigh wedged against her crotch, and moved her own leg between Star's out of instinct, craving and need.

When Imagine appeared on stage, she immediately noticed the fellow sitting in the same corner as he had the week before. This time he was dressed in jeans, a T-shirt and black leather jacket with matching motorcycle boots, but he was definitely the same guy. There was something immaculate about his appearance — the precise way his hair fell over his ears, and the way the shadow graced his cherubic features and smooth skin.

She knew that he bathed daily, unlike so many of their other patrons. She knew he was a professional, not some blue-collar worker that got drunk in the morning, then went in to build cars all day long with a flask in his hip pocket.

When she pulled off her teddy, she met his eyes, took a deep breath and expanded her chest to better show off her breasts . . .

What was she doing? This was a guy! A customer! Some mongrel who came in from the street like a piece of gum on her shoe. She looked away, withdrawing into herself, trying to allow the alcohol to work its magic, to transform her from Jennifer into Imagine.

Sweet little Jennifer Riddley could never stand on a stage, dancing, fucking poles, revealing herself to men. Jennifer Riddley was a good little politically correct lesbian from a Roman Catholic household where words like *dyke* were never used.

Only Imagine could strip for males, tease them with her full breasts and long legs, show them what she was and flirt with them. Imagine, her daring alter-ego, could do what needed to be done, could stand the feel of stranger's hands on her legs, her stomach, her breasts. Jennifer Riddley was incapable of that — in fact, incapable of true passion or love or even lust, according to two of her exes.

She spun on her heel away from the gawking men, unable to face them while thoughts of her last ex, Margaret, trailed through her mind. The way Margaret touched her, dipped her fingers inside her, kissed her lips, her breasts, her . . . her cunt.

The way Margaret finally said that she couldn't compete with the thrills Imagine gave her. She couldn't stand thinking of Jennifer dancing for men in some bar, taking her clothes off in front of total strangers.

That was four months ago, just before her twenty-second birthday. Four months and still Jennifer wasn't over the two-year relationship. She brought a hand up to her cheek, to wipe away the tear there, before turning to once again face the crowd.

She very rarely lapsed into Jennifer when she was onstage — her facade of Imagine was almost total. But in this moment when she was totally exposed, physically, emotionally and mentally — she looked up and met his eyes.

His gaze was on her. And it was clear he knew something was going on with her.

He understood.

In that single moment, she felt more naked than ever before.

She tried to pull her gaze from him, but they were locked together in some sort of strange dance, his dark eyes leading her while she spun and ran her hands over her body. Meanwhile, she teetered between Imagine and Jennifer, unable to keep up the persona of the luscious dancer that she had worked so hard to create. She had momentarily allowed him within the shell, and he wasn't letting go.

But it wasn't until two weeks later, his fourth Friday, that he waved a bill as she exited the stage. By this time, she was accustomed to his searching gaze, his craving looks — looks that saw beyond the front she put up for her customers.

He was becoming an old friend by the time he waved the bill.

She wasn't sure if she was afraid or eager when she saw that brief flash of green from the back table in the smoke-filled bar. She only knew she couldn't turn it down.

Wearing only a g-string and heels —she had stopped wearing the fishnet stockings because of too many dreams of his hands on her naked thighs — she approached him and thrust her pelvis forward so he could deposit the —

She sucked in her breath. There was a hundred-dollar bill in her g-string. She had never before received such a tip for a simple lap dance.

She lifted herself up onto his muscular legs.

"Come home with me," he hoarsely whispered toward her, his hands resting lightly on her legs.

"I can't do that," she said, placing her hands on his shoulders.

He looked up at her, and she was finally able to see that his eyes were brown — the brown velveteen of an old teddy bear. She lowered herself to gently brush her lips against his.

He arched up to meet her kiss, possessing her mouth as if it were his for the asking. Jennifer pulled away, afraid of the feelings this . . . this *man* was bringing about in her. They stared at each other, just breathing in each other's essence.

His hands slowly began caressing her thighs, moving from the outside to the inside, before they reached up, caressing her ass, fingering the thin line of her g-string and spreading over her stomach.

Jennifer grabbed wildly at the persona of Imagine to pull her through this, but she knew it was Jennifer that arched up at his touch. She knew she wanted him, wanted him with the eternal hard bulge in his pants.

She had never seen him this closely before — the short black hair streaked with gray, the blackish/grayish five o'clock shadow, the almost too smooth skin . . .

He cupped and caressed her breasts, defying the law that dictated what the men receiving lap dances could do to her, how they could touch her, but she was unable to stop him. Instead she was mesmerized by his face, his eyes. Those brown orbs held a softness she could've only imagined.

The hands that caressed her body were delicate, the long fingers unmarred by calluses, amazingly thin, slender even. His features were finely cut, aristocratic maybe. His dark beard reached almost to his hairline, just above his ears, but not quite.

As his lips caressed her extended nipple, while his

hands moved back down over her g-string, reaching toward a hidden place between her thighs, she arched toward his touch and dropped her fingers toward his beard, running her thumbs over it . . .

She felt his thumbs pushing the thin line of her g-string aside, pulling her shaven lips apart, running up and down her slick clit, and she brought her hands up to the light: there was a darkness tinting the flesh. She looked down at his beard and realized there were trails where her fingers and thumbs had lain.

Suddenly understanding, she reached down and undid the fly of his trousers, pushing down the boxer shorts even as he entered her, pushing his fingers into her while she moaned her appreciation.

When Jennifer released the pink rubber dildo, the woman grinned up at her. "I didn't misjudge you, did I?"

All too aware of the customers at the tables around her, Jennifer slipped herself onto the dildo, letting it slowly fill her while she took it all in. She rode it, up and down, until she collapsed against this woman in drag. "Come home with me tonight," she whispered in relief.

Quiet Place

Karin Kallmaker

The noise level in the anteroom had grown to an unbearable level. I seized the ring bearer and flower girl by the scruffs of their respective necks and shook once. "That's enough! Do you want Pam and Sheri to hear you?"

The two *enfants terribles* subsided and the noise level was more manageable. The attending party of bridesmaids and bridesmen was loud enough without little Greg and Cindy playing the "I'm not touching you" game at the tops of their lungs.

Pam's mother, Marcia, bustled in with her checklist. She was very much the presiding dowager in her gray silk gown and double stand of pearls.

"Doreen, why isn't everyone lined up?"

"I was just going to suggest that we get ready." I stepped to one side as my attempt at order was no long needed. Marcia would manage everything, and I was happy with that.

The room fell silent, and the attending party took their places. Pam had won a coin toss with Sheri that put me, her bridesmaid of honor, at the front of the line. Behind me was Sheri's bridesman of honor, Philip. Behind Philip came Pam's next dearest friend, then Sheri's, and so on for a total of ten. Marcia checked me over, tweaked a bit of lace to a point on my shoulder where it scratched more, and moved on to her next victim. From Philip's near choke I gathered Marcia had cinched in either his tie or his cummerbund.

I didn't begrudge Marcia her attention to detail. As the bridesmaid of honor, I had had far more to do than I could handle. I had thrown one heck of a bridal shower, helped the other attendants schedule their fittings, found a shop to dye the women's shoes and managed *les enfants*. On top of grading my end-of-semester papers and finals, it hadn't been easy. Ordinarily, it wouldn't have been that hard, but my mind had been in turmoil from the moment Pam had told me, seemingly out of the blue, she and Sheri were going to tie the knot. In retrospect, I just hadn't wanted to know it was coming.

When I had pled lack of time for other details, Marcia had been happy to take over. In fact, having assumed she would not be given the opportunity to participate in a wedding for her lesbian and only daughter, Marcia had been ecstatic to visit a hundred caterers, search through dozens of bridal stores and evaluate cakes, stemware, chair and table rentals and so on.

Marcia was the reason the "holy union" had gone from "simple and family only" to a splashy affair with all the trimmings. Pam and Sheri had protested at first, but I watched them both get caught up in selecting gowns and flowers and hors d'oeuvres. Even some lesbians, it seemed, wanted white weddings. The idea had never crossed my mind. I thought bitterly that it should have. I had not known Pam nearly as well as I had supposed.

Sheri's mother had died several years ago, and there had been no mothers-of-the-brides competition. The fathers-of-the-brides had been happy to step back and look generally affable.

We passed Marcia's inspection. As we shared a collective sigh of relief, the door to the inner room opened and Pam and Sheri stepped out.

The others oohed and aahed, but my breath froze in my breast. Pam was radiant, truly radiant. Her high cheekbones were stained with red, and her deep blue eyes shimmered between laughter and tears. She had always been elegantly tall, but the Elizabethan-style dress, with its waist set low on her hips, emphasized her slenderness and added yet more grace to a figure that already danced when she walked. Her long arms were encased in three-quarter-length white gloves, leaving her shoulders and throat bare above the form-fitting bodice of the gown. Lavender and silver roses were set in her black hair.

I wanted to step backward, but there was no room behind me. The air trembled with emotion and I felt lightheaded. Sheri was dressed in the same style of dress with salmon and silver roses in her hair. To my eyes, Sheri didn't look half as fine as Pam. I told myself to let it go. I reminded myself that I liked and respected Sheri.

But I only had eyes for Pam. I'd known her since I was fourteen. When we'd moved to Ann Arbor, I hadn't known anyone. Pam had made me welcome in choir and helped me conjugate French verbs. She was two months younger, but I would always think of her as older. She was certainly more sophisticated and a better instructor. She would not be standing there on my wedding day thinking my choice of life mate was inferior.

But then, Pam was not in love with me.

The organ was striking the opening chords of the elegiac Bach piece for the processional, and I tore my gaze from the excited rise and fall of Pam's breast as she said something to Sheri. I hadn't seen the fathers enter, and they each proffered a jewel case to their respective daughter. Pam's dad had tears in his eyes as she ducked her head to allow him to fasten the gold chain around her neck. The lapis lazuli pendant seemed to tremble in the light as it settled on her bare chest. Sheri's pendant looked like carnelian, but I could not bring myself to gather around and admire either stone.

"Everyone needs to get back in line." Marcia gestured with great authority. Within moments we were orderly again. I could smell Philip's cologne as he stood behind me. I closed my eyes for a moment, and the vision Pam made was brilliant behind my closed lids.

The parents left the anteroom and proceeded somberly through the foyer. Marcia signaled me before stepping into the aisle. I moved forward and the other attendants followed. To hide my shaking hands, I dug my gloved fingers into the rose bouquet I carried. I glanced at the dressing mirror just inside the door and did not recognize myself. My face was pallid and my makeup seemed to sit on top of my skin.

I prayed that everyone would assume I had stage fright.

It was the hardest thing I've ever done. Right, together, left, together. I knew Philip was right behind me, but there was no one between me and the altar, and I felt as if I was walking to Judgment Day.

At the bottom of the nave steps, I moved to the left on Pam's side of the aisle, and Philip sidled to the right to start the row of Sheri's attendants. Once the train that had followed me divided up, we turned and faced the door. The organist began "Here Comes the Bride."

Greg's little face was scrunched up with the concentration required to balance the pillow bearing two heavy gold rings. Right behind him was Cindy, happily strewing the contents of her basket — lavender, salmon and silver rose petals.

Greg and Cindy were nearly at the altar when Pam and Sheri entered, each carrying a magnificent bouquet of roses. The whisper of their gowns was lost in the collective *aah* of the assembled guests. Everyone rose.

Pam and Sheri had tears in their eyes as they favored guests on each side of the aisle with smiles and whispered greetings.

I only had eyes for Pam. I didn't know that tears were spilling down my face until Marcia leaned out of the front pew to slip me a handkerchief. She'd told me she had a ready supply because everybody cried for joy at weddings.

The minister came down the steps of the nave to meet the brides, then turned and led them up the shallow steps so they were before the altar. He blessed them, and everyone knelt in prayer.

It was finally quiet. In the silence, broken only by the minister's words of divine blessing and the power of love, I could hear the roaring in my ears. It was like the sound of an earthquake, the rending of two bonded elemental forces. My quiet place, where I usually found reflection and sustenance, was filled with the sound of my heart breaking.

I sat next to my first-ever girl date. Pam and her girlfriend had arranged our meeting. We kept our gaze fixed on the drive-in movie screen. I could hear the quick intake of Pam's breath in the back seat as she and her girlfriend ignored the movie — ignored us, too. I was flushed and shaking and trying to hide it, but Pam moaned with a mixture of surprise and anticipation. The sound of her in that other girl's arms brought pain and pleasure. I could pretend it was my mouth nuzzling her breasts, my tongue tasting the salt on her skin. While I pretended it was almost as good as reality.

I rose only because the person next to me did. How could I still be standing by, watching her with

other women, and not yet have found a way to tell
her how I felt? I had always thought there would be
time. Time for her to see me as another woman, not
her best chum from high school. Time for a moment
when her eyes saw the yearning in mine.

"Who brings these women to the beginning of
their new life?"

The parents stood and murmured in unison, "We
do."

The minister addressed the congregation. "Is there
anyone present with any knowledge of why these two
women should not enter into a new life together?"

I froze. In the split second it takes to dream, I
heard my dream-self shriek, "I do!"

I do!

But the rest of the words would not even come to
mind, let alone be spoken aloud. I'd been denying
them from the moment I'd seen the way Pam looked
at Sheri — the way she never looked at me. What
was the point of saying what I felt for Pam when I
could not say the other half of the line? I could not
say, "And she loves me."

The minister was giving Pam and Sheri words of
wisdom about give and take, then spoke to Pam
alone.

"Do you, Pam, take Sheri to be your wife and
mate, to respect and cherish, to trust and honor, in
sickness and in health, for richer or poorer, in
darkness and in light for the rest of your life?"

Pam looked unflinchingly into Sheri's eyes. "I do
swear it, with all my heart."

My little moan was lost in Marcia's choked sob.
Why was Marcia crying, I wondered. What loss of

hers could possibly compare to mine? I wasn't just losing Pam, I was losing my cherished vision of a future with Pam in it.

My ears were deaf to Sheri's vows, then Greg stepped forward and offered the rings to the minister. Pam and Sheri removed their gloves and draped them on the pillow and Greg stepped back to fidget and pick at his pants.

The two bands of gold were blessed, then the minister removed the thin lavender ribbon from one and handed it to Pam.

Pam's voice never wavered. "With this ring, I bond with you forever. I promise to listen, to speak and above all to love." She slipped the ring onto Sheri's finger. It was a perfect fit.

The minister untied the salmon ribbon on the second ring and gave the ring to Sheri.

Sheri's voice was low and intense. "With this ring, I pledge my heart and soul to you for the rest of my life. Every day I will hope that time stops so our lives together can truly be eternal."

Marcia sobbed loudly into her husband's shoulder, and a soft murmur of kind laughter and satisfaction rippled through the congregation. All I saw was the band of gold on Pam's finger. The minister happily suggested that they seal their vows with a kiss. Pam laughed with delight and offered her mouth to Sheri.

I felt her laugh in my ear, made more intimate by the whisper of her breath across my cheek. Her lips were soft, and my body trembled at the closeness of her. I lifted my mouth — I breathed in her kiss and reveled in her love . . .

Hoots from the audience brought the two of them

out of their embrace. It was done. Pam was still my friend, and I bitterly hoped I never saw her again. We hurried down the aisle in the wake of the brides and into the reception hall. Marcia miraculously arrived ahead of everyone and began directing people this way and that. I kept on going, my gown trailing on the damp grass outside the reception hall. My custom-dyed shoes were quickly blotched and ruined. Like the dress I wore, they weren't meant to be used again, but preserved for some future time when I wanted to remember this day.

In the garden I found a secluded bench and collapsed. I pressed Marcia's handkerchief to my face and let the long, racking cries break out of me at last.

The shadows had deepened by the time I forced myself to get up. I knew there wasn't a shred of makeup left on my face, and my eyes felt as if they would never fully open again. I crept around to the back of the church and found a tiny rest room where I could lock myself in. The distant sounds of the celebration seeped under the door.

I looked like hell and even then I didn't look as miserable as I felt. I washed my face and pressed the cold, damp handkerchief to my eyes for a few minutes.

A soft knock at the door startled me.

"Who is it?"

"Philip."

I opened the door slightly.

He offered a glass of Champagne. "I saw you cross the lawn and thought you could use this."

I accepted the glass. When he didn't retreat, I

opened the door sufficiently for him to slip into the tiny room with me.

"Thanks," I said. My throat was beyond parched. I drained the glass and then filled it with water and drained it again.

Philip watched me with a look in his eyes I took for pity. His were almost as bloodshot as mine.

"I wouldn't have said you were the type to cry at weddings," I said by way of filling the awkward silence that had engulfed the small space. "Not after your eloquence about the outdated nature of the institution and the oppressive burden of the heterosexual model which you, as a heterosexual, had no intention of supporting."

He half smiled, far more pain than pleasure. "For all the good it did. They were pledging fidelity and happily-ever-after anyway."

"It hardly seems worth it to vow 'until we no longer feel like it.' "

"Statistically, that's closer to the truth for almost fifty percent of marriages."

"You think they don't love each other? That it won't last?" I didn't dare hope. If ever Pam needed me I would be there for her. But I could not, would not, wish her and Sheri ill.

He didn't answer right away. "I don't know why Sheri and Pam would be the . . . lucky ones."

"Because they do love each other," I said in a whisper.

"How can you be sure?"

The pain of my own heart made me sure. I knew I had lost her forever. "I just am."

He sighed. "So am I."

I turned to the mirror and made one last daub at my ravaged face. My gaze met his in the mirror — and I finally recognized the similarity.

"We're a pair of losers, aren't we?"

Philip inhaled deeply. "How can you lose what you never had?"

"I only want her to be happy."

"She's not good enough for her."

"I don't know what you see in her."

We laughed ruefully at our similarly partisan sentiments, then Philip offered to find some more Champagne. Poor Philip. I felt almost as sorry for him as I did for myself. But not quite as much — he hadn't lost Pam.

The lighting at the reception had dimmed, and the dancing was spirited. I hadn't eaten since my hasty lunch but recklessly accepted the Champagne Philip offered. We danced, trying not to be obvious about our preoccupation with Pam and Sheri, who swayed together as if bonded from the breast down.

I was nibbling on puffy cheese cardboard when Pam appeared next to me.

"I wanted to say thank you before we left. I couldn't have done it without you."

The Champagne helped me meet her happy smile with some sort of smile of my own. "It was a beautiful ceremony."

"I saw you dancing with Philip." Her eyes were bright with suggestion.

I had not thought I could feel more wounded. Why didn't she just rip my fingernails past the quick or paper-cut my heart? It's the minor wounds and thoughtless words that hurt the most. "*He* is not my type, you know that."

Her brightness dimmed slightly. "I know. It's just . . . I'm so happy. I want you to be, too. And you've never —"

"You don't know everything about me, Pam." I had hid my feelings so well that she even doubted I was a lesbian. How pathetic. I'd gone out, even indulged my libido, but I'd never talked about anyone else to Pam. I hadn't wanted her to think there was anyone else. There was no one else.

"I know you have your own life. I've been so wrapped up in the wedding that you could have had a dozen girls and I wouldn't have noticed."

I could see she had no idea that she was killing me by inches.

She went on blithely, "I don't want this to make a difference between us, Dori. Sheri and I are committed to not disappearing into some couple funk and losing all our friends."

She was in earnest, I could tell, which made me hate her. How could she not know how I felt? How could she not see the truth of it in my face, my eyes?

She whispered, "If only you had said something. I'd given up hope. She's just second-best. No one will ever compare to you. But now it's too late. Too late . . ."

"We're going to be late to the airport," she was saying. She signaled Sheri that she'd be just one more minute. "So call me when I get back, okay?"

She would be bronzed from the Jamaican sun.

She would be even lovelier, even more in love. "Sure."

Never.

I hung to the back when everyone gathered outside the church to see the brides off on their honeymoon. The cynicism I now shared with Philip about Forever After made me put my hands behind my back as the bouquets were tossed. Pam's bounced off my head, and someone else caught it before it hit the ground.

With pounds of birdseed whizzing through the air, the limousine finally pulled away from the curb.

In the morning Pam would stir and find Sheri next to her, just as she had yesterday and just as she would next week, next year. I was always alone by morning. I was usually alone at night. Now even being alone was ruined. My quiet place was full of losing her.

How can you lose what you never had?

I knew that answer. It's easy. You just stand there.

Now or Never

Laura DeHart Young

C'mon, Jamie! You can do it!"

"It's now or never, Jamie! Jump!"

She looked down at the four heads bobbing in the water. Even her seven-year-old brother, Logan, had jumped. Mom was going to kill them all when she found out. Looking around, she saw the mountains bathed in summer sun. The blue of the sky reflected onto the surface of the water where the heads still bobbed like porous driftwood logs, waiting for her to find the courage. Her brothers had made jumping from this mountain ledge near their upper New York State vacation home a summer ritual. Always frightened, she had watched them soar again and again like graceful birds until they landed in the lake below, cutting the surface like the blades of a motorboat.

This was not the first time her brothers had dared her to jump. Secretly, she had always wanted to try. But as many times as she had climbed the brambled slope to the high rocky ledge, just as many times she had quit. Always, at the last moment, fear took hold and she would back away from the challenge. Now, at the ripe old age of twelve, she had run out of excuses.

"Jamie," Logan yelled. "It's like flying. Don't be afraid. We're right here!"

Suddenly, she was in the air, Logan's words still skipping through her brain. If he could find the courage, so could she. For a brief second, her momentum catapulted her above the ledge, then she began to float down toward the gleaming water. Arms stretched outward, she duplicated the swan dive her brothers had taught her at the local swimming pool. Logan was right. It was like flying. In an instant she captured the sky, mountains and water in her vision and held them there, swooping like a bird into the center of it all. At the last moment, she brought her arms together, stiffened her body and felt her hands cut the water's surface. She rocketed through the water until finally she stopped about ten feet below. She kicked hard, propelling herself back toward the sunlight. Her brothers met her reappearance with cheers and hugs. Her heart was bursting with joy.

"Jamie, you did it!" She lifted Logan into her arms. She could feel his ribs under his wet skin.

"Isn't it just like flying, sis? Isn't it?"

"Yes, it is. C'mon, little guy, your lips are turning blue. Mom's going to kill us anyway, so we might as well go inside and get it over with."

"Do we have to tell her? Do we? She won't let me swim anymore," Logan protested.

Jamie looked at Logan, then at the rest of her brothers. "Can we keep this a secret?"

In unison, they all nodded. And the secret was kept for many years.

From that day on, it was Logan who taught her courage, who reminded her that life was short and that she should cherish every opportunity and face challenges without fear. Logan, who was told he would never see his twentieth birthday due to the cystic fibrosis that ravaged his lungs, had an enduring notion that guided his every decision: "Now or never." It was that same indomitable spirit that helped him endure the daily physical therapy. Jamie was, at first, hesitant to pound her brother's back so vigorously that he shook with coughing spasms.

"Harder," he would scold her.

Hands cupped, she would pound his back and chest until tears streamed down her face. Somehow,

124 THE VERY THOUGHT OF YOU

his small frame survived the pounding and he always ended up comforting her.

"It's okay, Jamie. I'm used to it, and I can finally get a deep breath when we're done."

During a break in the second semester of her senior year in college, Jamie flew from Virginia to New York City to spend time with her family and Logan. Well into his teens, Logan was filled with an elation for life that was infectious. He had just learned to drive and offered to take her for a spin in his new, used Chevy pickup truck.

"Well, what do you think, sis?" he asked, his sandy blond hair tousled in curls around his stubbled face.

"Of your driving, the new truck or the beard you're trying to grow?"

Logan threw back his head and laughed. His blue eyes sparkled mischievously. "Maybe you better not comment on anything!"

"Maybe not. But I would like your comments on something. Something important."

"Hey, no problem."

"What would you think if I told you I was a lesbian?"

Logan was silent. He pulled the truck off to the shoulder of the road. Finally, he looked at her and said, "Really?"

Jamie felt an adrenaline rush of fear. "Yes, really."

"Gosh, how do you know something like that?"

"You just know."

Logan nodded in agreement. He sat for a few moments, seemingly deep in thought, his hands still clutching the steering wheel. "And you want to know what I think of this?" he asked with a puzzled expression.

"Does it bother you?"

"Not at all," he said matter-of-factly. "Although I don't see that it matters much what I think. But, if you really want to know, I say life doesn't wait, Jamie. Be happy." He looked at her and smiled. "Are you happy?"

"Yes, very." Relieved to have her brother's support, Jamie quickly said, "Now drive us to our favorite ice cream stand and treat me to a large chocolate cone."

Logan revved up the engine. "Yeah, what a great idea. Definitely my treat."

Just after Jamie turned twenty-four, Logan suffered through a lengthy hospital stay due to pneumonia. When he was finally released, Jamie volunteered to take Logan to visit his primary-care doctor. Her mother and father, who had kept a constant vigil during Logan's hos- pitalization, needed a break. She and her brothers sent them to the Jersey shore for a week's vacation.

Now in the latter stages of CF, Logan was about to begin the use of an experimental drug, which promised to reduce Logan's frequency of lung infec- tions — and also to improve his overall lung function.

Jamie was surprised when the office door opened.

She had expected to see Dr. Robert Thomason, Logan's pulmonary specialist who had been treating his CF for almost twenty years. Instead, a striking woman, with chestnut brown hair barely touching the shoulders of her long white coat, entered the room. She smiled broadly at both of them, her steely gray eyes resting a moment longer on Jamie.

"Hi, I'm Dr. Woods," she said, turning back toward Logan. "You must be Logan Reed."

Logan shook the doctor's hand. "Hi, Doc. This is my sister, Jamie."

Dr. Woods picked up a clipboard and nodded again in her direction. "Jamie, nice to meet you." Leaning the palm of her hand on the end of the exam table, Dr. Woods continued with absolutely no pretense. "Dr. Thomason is out of town at a CF convention." She turned back to Logan. "But I've been studying your file, Logan. I've consulted with Doctor Thomason on beginning the use of this new drug. There's a chance of getting some good results. What do you think?"

"Hey, let's get started then," Logan said enthusiastically. "I've got things to do."

"I see," the doctor said with a laugh. After listening to Logan's lungs, she gave him some sample packages of the medication and explained the dosage and possible side effects. "Any questions?"

"Not right now," Logan said, turning one of the packages over in his hands. "Seems simple enough."

"Good. I'll walk you both out."

Dr. Woods opened the door, and Logan walked ahead of them down the narrow corridor. As always, Logan stopped to flirt with every nurse at the main desk. While Jamie waited, Dr. Woods lingered by her side.

"How does your brother seem to be doing overall?" she asked in a tone that suggested genuine concern.

"He's tough," Jamie answered softly. "I don't know how he keeps going."

"Listen, if you have any questions about the medication, or anything at all, call me. Okay?"

"Thanks. I will."

A week later, Jamie was in the supermarket two blocks from her apartment. She stuffed naval oranges into a plastic bag, twirled it and tied it shut.

"How are you?"

Jamie felt a hand on her shoulder. She swung around and was more than surprised to fall into the gaze of Dr. Woods. "Uh, hello. I'm fine, Dr. Woods. And you?"

"Running a few errands." The doctor pointed to the plastic basket that held a few vegetables. "Refrigerator's empty."

"I know the feeling."

"How's Logan?"

"Actually, he's doing pretty well. The new medication seems to be working."

"That's great news."

"Yes, it is."

Dr. Woods looked nervous. She shrugged and said, "I don't know if you'd be interested or not, but there's a great little café on the next block. I was going to stop in for a bite to eat. Care to join me?"

Jamie hesitated. She felt unsure. She had just been through a failed relationship. Then, as though Logan were standing there beside her at that very moment, she heard the soft whisper of his voice: *"Now or never, sis."* Jamie closed her eyes, thinking she was half crazy. Then she quickly gathered her wits, looked at the doctor and smiled. "Yes, that would be very nice. But what about the food?"

Dr. Woods looked at her basket and then at Jamie's cart. She frowned. "Hmmm. Good point."

"Hey, my apartment's only two blocks from here. We can drop the food off, then have lunch."

"I love spontaneous women," Dr. Woods said with a warm smile.

"I think it was Logan who taught me the benefits of spontaneity."

"No doubt. By the way, you can call me Shera."

Lunch that day with Shera turned into candlelit dinners, movies and long walks in the Village. One humid evening, after a walk down Christopher Street and some light appetizers at a favorite sidewalk restaurant, the two women returned to Shera's townhouse.

Without so much as a word between them, they fell into each other's arms. Spontaneity had returned in the form of passion. Jamie brushed Shera's hair

away from her face and stared into those stormy gray
eyes. Her temples thumped from the rush of excitement as she kissed Shera, their tongues melting
together in one hot breath.

"How's my bedside manner?" Shera whispered.

"Not bad. Not bad at all."

There wasn't a single part of her body that did
not ache for Shera's touch. Jamie wrapped her arms,
thighs and even the tips of her toes around Shera,
wanting to feel every inch of Shera's warmth against
her own. She could smell the spicy aroma of Shera's
perfume, feel the soft layers of Shera's hair falling
across her breasts.

"I've wanted to do this for weeks," Shera said in
a husky stammer. Shera teasingly thumbed Jamie's
nipples, then took them one by one into her mouth.
Jamie responded in writhing delight as the soft lips
caressed each breast. In between the exhilarating
moments of arousal, there were deep kisses and
intimate glances that rocked Jamie's world.

Shera's tongue worked a slow, delirious magic
between Jamie's legs. At the same time, with the
forceful movement of her hips, Jamie drove Shera's
fingers deeper into the wetness that betrayed her
desire. A steep climb of pleasure, guided by a tenderness she had never known, ended in a wonderful
release of love and passion. Her body trembled in
Shera's arms and against the loving caresses that
came in the form of a hand across her cheek, soft
kisses along her neck, the rub of a foot along her
calf.

"How beautiful you are, Miss Reed."
"What a glorious lover you are, Dr. Woods."
"Beautiful and glorious together."

Three years later, when Logan was hospitalized for the final time, Jamie sat as his bedside for days, silently thanking him for so many things. His success in living a full lifetime in almost twenty-eight years had made her grateful for every moment she encountered. She took risks and accepted challenges, overcoming her innate shyness. At a time when she was unsteady, Logan's complete and matter-of-fact acceptance of her as a lesbian allowed her to openly celebrate who she was. And, as a direct result of his terrible illness, it was Logan's greatest joy to know that Jamie had met Shera, now her partner of three years.

"I guess the CF was good for something," he wheezed, smiling though the oxygen mask. "Man, you're happy. The shine in your eyes lights up the room."

"I would give that happiness back, if only —"

"Nope, sis," he interrupted. "No point thinking about what might have been or could be. Doesn't work that way." He coughed and sputtered, trying to talk. "I'm just so glad to see you happy. It makes me feel like I'm leaving something wonderful behind."

Tears stung her eyes. Her brother was dying — how could she possibly be happy?

As if reading her thoughts, Logan said, "No damned long drawn-out mourning, Jamie. Don't you understand that I've beaten this thing? I beat the odds long ago — and you damned well know it. You've got no idea how good that feels."

Jamie sat with Shera in her den, sipping a glass of wine. Outside the window, large flakes of snow covered the backyard in a blanket of white. In the background, Christmas music played. Logan had been gone for three months, and Jamie's heart still ached for a glimpse of his rugged good looks as he sauntered up her parents' driveway, the sound of his infectious laughter, the warmth of his gentle hugs. Still, he had left so much of himself behind and that's what she held onto.

Shera put her arm around Jamie. "I've been thinking about him too. I loved him very much."

"I know you did." Jamie leaned over and softly kissed Shera's cheek. "And thanks to Logan, we have our love for each another. As long as we have that, he'll always be here with us."

"Then he'll be with us forever."

Don't Think

Lyn Denison

I'm not the impulsive type. I've always hesitated in case I lost, looked before I leaped, stitched in time and saved nine. I guess you get my drift.

So I was standing with a drink in my hand, wishing I'd refused to come to Gwen's party, when I spotted an extremely striking woman, tall and dark, like Sandy. A few years ago I would have thought, she who hesitates is lost, and I'd have walked on over. But not now. I'd never been so confused about anything in my life.

Of course, it was all Gwen's fault. You see . . .

Maybe I should begin at the beginning. Well, I was born . . . Just joking.

Seriously, we have to go back about a year or so. One year, one month, two weeks, to be exact. That was the day I walked in on Sandy and Tina.

I had some flextime due, so without thinking I decided to head home from work early, take time making dinner, get out the scented candles, tempt Sandy into a bubble bath or something. We hadn't done anything romantic, let alone raunchy, in ages.

So I strolled home, stopped to talk to a neighbor, climbed the stairs and, unsuspecting, went inside. I put down my briefcase and walked into the bedroom to change. Nothing could have prepared me for the tangled nakedness of Sandy and Tina. I thought my heart had stopped beating. Sandy and I had been together for nearly three years.

The next thing I knew I was on Gwen's doorstep, a hastily packed suitcase in my hand. And Sandy's urgent apologies, her pleading, and then her anger were replaying over and over in my head.

"Well, what can you expect, Tash?" She'd spat out. "We've been living our lives by rote. It's boring. I feel like my life's been planned to the nth degree. For once I did something I didn't stop to think about. And it was fantastic. If you tried it we mightn't be having this conversation."

Gwen helped me get through the next few hours, days, weeks, months. I stayed in her spare room for a while, then she helped me find another flat.

I'll admit I wallowed a little. All right. I wallowed a lot. But I'm good at wallowing. I can even enjoy it. In retrospect.

So I went to work, I came home. I refused to go anywhere Gwen suggested I go, with or without her. I sat and thought about my sorry self.

Gwen still dropped in to see me every week, bringing food and videos, and despite myself I started looking forward to her visits. So much so that I actually heard myself agreeing to go to a small party she was having last weekend.

You see, Gwen and I went way back. We'd met at secondary school when we were about twelve and had been friends ever since. Apart from that one time when I was sixteen and I fell for Marielle Roberts. Gwen and I had our only fight about that.

"She's shallow," Gwen had said heartlessly.

"She's beautiful," I'd replied.

Gwen shook her head and walked away. I hung out with Marielle, and Gwen started dating Brett the Bountiful, who worked out like a footballer but was actually captain of the chess club and the debating team. About then Marielle kissed me and I stopped pretending I didn't prefer women.

When I got a bruised heart over Marielle, Gwen commiserated and we were friends again.

We went away to Uni together, and after we graduated Gwen went home to the country to teach and I stayed in the city. It was just after she left that I met Sandy, and Gwen and I lost touch for a while. Then Gwen called me to say she was transferred down to Brisbane and could she look me up. We picked up our friendship where we'd left off.

That was a couple of years ago. I'd been really excited to see her again. Sandy was soon sick of hearing about Gwen's and my youthful escapades.

"Are you certain you and this Gwen were never an item?" Sandy'd asked, irritated.

My jaw had dropped in surprise. "Gwen and I are best friends. And Gwen's straight."

"Are you sure?"

For some reason this had made me furious. "Of course I'm sure. She's been engaged since I've seen her. To a guy," I added for emphasis.

"She isn't engaged now," Sandy persisted.

"No. But there's Sam. Don't forget him." I got the last word in.

I sat and thought about this as I waited for the tall, dark woman I'd met at Gwen's party last weekend, my first date since Sandy.

Gwen had gone out with a couple of guys while I moped around over women. It was strange, but I couldn't remember actually telling Gwen I was a lesbian. Of all the things we did talk about over the years we'd never discussed our sexuality. That was weird. I frowned. Now, why —?

A knock on the door forced the thought out of my mind, and my stomach knotted nervously as I opened the door and smiled.

"Hi there! Ready?" Dark eyes full of promise and laced with challenge met mine.

"Sure," I said and wondered if I actually was. I had my gravest doubts, but it was too late now. Wasn't it?

We went to a local lesbian bar. I hadn't been there for ages and it crossed my mind that I might run into Sandy. I gave that some thought and decided, as our community wasn't all that big, I'd have to see her sometime so it might as well be now. Maybe I was over her, I told myself. *Maybe?* I had a pretty fair idea I had been for some time.

Two hours later I climbed out of a cab and looked up at the lighted window. She was home. Maybe I should have phoned. But what would I have said? I paused for a moment, almost getting back into the taxi, but I paid the fare and then ran up the steps, knocked on the door.

Gwen gazed at me in surprise, her eyes looking behind me, obviously checking to see if I was alone.

"Tash? What's wrong?"

I laughed naturally for the first time in a long while. "Nothing's wrong." I peered into her flat. "Am I interrupting?" I asked, and it occurred to me that Sam might be there. I wondered why I could suddenly hear my heartbeats echoing in my ears.

"Interrupting? No. Not unless you count resorting my CDs as 'anything,' " Gwen said wryly and motioned me inside. "Want some coffee? Tea?" She raised her eyebrows. "Something stronger?"

"Coffee would be nice," I said and followed her into the kitchen.

Gwen was shorter than I was, had more curves. I was concentrating on them and nearly measured my length as I tripped over Max, Gwen's spoiled moggy. He rubbed up against my legs, and I picked him up and gave him a hug.

"He can take all of this I can give him," I said as Max began to purr like a steam engine.

"Can you blame him?" Gwen laughed.

She must have just brewed a pot of coffee because

she filled two mugs, added milk and sugar to mine, and we walked back into the living room. We settled down in opposite chairs, Max curling up on my lap.

"Didn't you have a hot date tonight?" Gwen asked casually, cautiously sipping her coffee.

"Turned lukewarm."

Gwen raised her eyebrows again. "How so? I thought you were keen."

"It was a false alarm." I shrugged.

Gwen looked across at me, and a burning sensation began in the pit of my stomach, and then started to wash over the rest of me. I felt sort of —

I looked away. Must be the coffee, I thought. I took another sip. Yes, had to be the coffee.

"I was under the impression you liked Kat," Gwen continued. "As in, very much."

"Oh, I did. I do," I said quickly and made a show of stroking Max. Gwen had told me Kat was a friend of a friend. "We went over to Rosie's," I added when a short silence seemed to gather more heavily around us. "They've got a new jukebox."

"Have they?"

I nodded. "Kat said she met you at Rosie's a couple of weeks ago and that's when you invited her to your party last weekend."

Gwen murmured noncommittally.

"She said you were with a couple of lesbians from the north coast." For the first time since we were teenagers I saw a faint color wash Gwen's cheeks.

"They'd just moved to Brisbane and wanted to meet other women."

"Oh," I said and swallowed, my mind racing at a hundred miles an hour in a lot of directions it had never been before. Well, not consciously. But I was beginning to think it had taken a few journeys while I wasn't paying attention. "I guess Rosie's was the place to take them," I added and thought Gwen relaxed a little.

What if —? Don't even think it, I told myself. Yes, but what if —?

"I thought Sam might be here?" I said, looking about the room as though he was about to materialize.

"Sam?" Gwen seemed to be searching her memory. "Oh, Sam. No. He moved away. That was months ago."

"Were you upset?" I was ashamed I didn't know. I'd been so wrapped up in my own misery over Sandy I hadn't even considered Gwen might be nursing her own broken heart.

"Upset? When Sam moved away?" Gwen shook her head. "Not really. We were just friends."

"You weren't sleeping with him?"

Gwen did go red then and seemed to be having trouble answering me.

"Was that too personal?" I asked, realizing we'd never broached this subject either, not on an individual level.

"No," Gwen said carefully. "And we weren't."

We were silent again, and I continued to stroke the cat. What if —? I pushed the thought away again. Between the thought I wasn't to think about and the hot coffee, I felt as though I were going to ignite.

"We've never talked about sex, have we?" I said, taking myself by surprise, and I grew warmer.

"No, we haven't." Gwen lifted her coffee mug to

her lips, using both hands, and she took a quick sip. "So, what do you want to know?" she asked, her blue eyes dancing, and I wrinkled my nose.

"About guys and the sleeping therewith?"

Gwen shrugged. "Guys. Gals. My knowledge knows no bounds. Theoretically. Now, when it comes to the practical application, well, I'm on shakier ground."

I laughed. "Aren't we all. Well, except maybe Barbie Thomasen. Remember her? If all she said was true then she was the *Guinness Book of Records"* *most sexually experienced sixteen-year-old."*

Gwen laughed, too. "You know she married the Lord Mayor's son?"

I gaped. "She did? When?"

"Not long after we graduated. Last count they had three kids. Didn't I tell you?"

"No." I shook my head. "That's unbelievable. I suppose most of the kids in our year left town like we did. There weren't many jobs to be had around there."

"Some stayed. And all of those are married." Gwen put her coffee mug on the table. "As far as I know we're the only two who aren't."

I looked away again, gave Max a ruffle. "Don't tell me Marielle Roberts got married."

Gwen paused. "Actually, she did. To Brett the Bountiful."

I was totally flummoxed. "She must have grown out of it."

Gwen picked up her coffee again, her fingers absently rubbing the pattern on the mug. I had the feeling she was a little disconcerted.

"You think you can do that? Grow out of it?" she asked with a studied casualness.

I pulled a self-derisive face. "Some of us don't," I said lightly, and she remained silent. "We've never talked about this either, have we?" I swallowed, my body hot again. "Why do you think that is?"

I watched, fascinated, as the pulse at the base of her throat began to throb wildly.

"We're talking about it now," she said, and she swallowed the way I'd just done.

Our eyes met.

"You know tonight I was sitting at Rosie's with Kat and I looked around and I asked myself why I was there. Why I was sitting opposite Kat. Why I was struggling to find something to say to her."

Gwen was inspecting the inside of her coffee mug now. "She seemed to make quite an impression on you last weekend."

"Everyone told me she did. And I'll admit she was attractive and sexy but —" I shrugged again.

"But what?" Gwen prompted.

"But I was sitting there and I suddenly realized I was thinking I didn't want to be with her. I wanted to be with someone else."

Gwen sighed. "Maybe it's too soon then. After Sandy."

"Not Sandy," I said. I wondered why she couldn't hear my heart thumping away triple time. "I was over Sandy quite a while ago."

"You were?"

I nodded. Gwen's eyes met mine, and I held my breath as I searched for the message I was desperately hoping was there. Should I take the chance?

If I was wrong the whole fabric of our lives would be rent, in tatters.

And then Gwen moved, pushed herself to the front of the couch, deliberately set her coffee mug on the table. She reached across, took my hand in hers. "Tash, there's something I want to tell you. I should have told you ages ago. But I didn't want to — I didn't think you'd — Do you think —?"

"Don't think, Gwen," I said thickly and dislodged the cat who protested noisily, stalking off in high dudgeon. Before I could think myself, I gently pulled Gwen forward and kissed her.

I slid my arms around her, moved my hands over her beautiful body. We were tangled together on the couch, my fingers under her shirt, her hands in my hair, both of us way out of control.

We kissed again, deep and long, and we were breathless when we finally moved slightly apart. My hands cupped Gwen's full breasts, settled on her waist, and we looked at each other.

"Am I dreaming this?" I asked softly, and she smiled that small wry smile I knew so well.

"I hope not. Although *I've* been dreaming this dream for so many years."

"You have? But what about, well, Sam? Your engagement? And Brett the Bountiful?" I asked.

"The Brett era was —" She grimaced. "I don't know. Maybe defense. Or just me trying to deny I wanted you like crazy. As to the engagement, that was a mistake. Luckily I realized it was before I did any more damage to him or to myself. And, as I said, Sam was just a friend."

I thought about what she'd said. Now I came to

think about it, since she'd returned to Brisbane there
had only been Sam. She hadn't dated anyone else I
knew of. Then I thought about something more.

"Have you —?"

"Dated other women?" She gave a quick laugh.
"In the old hometown? Not likely." She paused and
then looked at me seriously. "No, I haven't. Do you
think you can bear to take on a complete novice?"

"Oh, I think I can," I said and kissed her again.

Special Delivery
Linda Hill

I can't wait to get home and get out of these clothes." Janet O'Conner took her gaze off the road just long enough to rub the back of her hand across her brow. It was hot. Too hot. And to make matters worse, the air conditioning in the truck wasn't working. She planned on giving Jimmy an earful when she got back to the station.

She had thought she'd get some relief when she made the delivery back at the Miller place. But the air under the shade of the huge pines had been stagnant and provided little more than a brief respite from the slow baking she'd received in the truck.

Just one more delivery and she'd be on her way home to the long cool shower that awaited. She took a right onto Cottage Road and tried not to give in to the usual envy. This was by far her favorite street in the community. All of the houses were less than ten years old, each nestled in the center of its own acre lot. Care had been taken to leave most of the older trees in place, a fact that made the country road all the more appealing.

Every lawn was manicured. Every bush and shrub strategically located and trimmed just so. Large, in-ground pools dotted nearly every backyard, each with its own fence for privacy. Janet wrinkled her nose as she eyed one pool then the next. Nearly every one was empty.

"Why bother having a pool if you don't use it on a day like today?" she muttered under her breath as a trickle of sweat slipped between her breasts. She thought about the apartment she rented and tried not to get depressed. "Just one more year," she reminded herself.

She missed having her own home. Missed planting her gardens, mowing the lawn, and even raking the leaves. But she didn't regret letting Susan keep the house when they broke up. She never could have lived there alone. Not after nearly twenty years with the love of her life.

A loud *harrumph* left her lips as she shifted into a higher gear. Susan's new lover had moved in within months of her leaving, and the thought still brought acid to her tongue. Susan had bought out Janet's half of the house, but with the rising cost of real estate, Janet's share hadn't been enough to buy the home she really wanted. So she'd waited, saving every penny over the next four years. *Just one more year.* She'd soon have enough to make an ample down payment.

As she checked the address on the package on the seat beside her, a thought occurred to her. Maybe she'd look for a house right here on this street. She would certainly see to it that *her* pool saw plenty of use. The thought made her smile. Distracted, she nearly missed the driveway of number 118, and the brakes of the truck squealed. She glanced up at the house, recognizing it as one that had been for sale the last time she'd driven by. But the sign in the front yard had vanished, meaning that a new family had taken up residence.

She eased the truck into the long driveway and let it roll forward several yards before applying the parking brake. Methodically, she grabbed the clipboard from the dash and noted the routing number of the package. She compared it with the number on the package itself and swore under her breath when she realized that this was a special delivery. Signature required. She hated it when she had to get a signature. Nine times out of ten it meant that she would have to leave a notice and return the next day. It was inevitably a wasted trip.

Sighing, she rolled back the door and stepped outside, retrieving the clipboard and the small package. The heat of the sun burned her neck. *Damn, it was hot.*

She made her way along the front walk and

pressed a finger to the doorbell. The worst part about delivering on this road — other than having to look at all of the pools, that is — was that she never knew which door to go to. There were so many. Front door. Side door. Garage door. Breezeway door. Back door. And in this case, when no one answered the bell, she was faced with a dilemma. Should she just leave the usual note, or should she go around back and try a different door?

What she really wanted to do was go home, but the Girl Scout in her wouldn't let her leave without at least trying one more time. So, tucking the package under one arm, she adjusted her sunglasses and made her way around the corner to the back of the house.

The first thing she heard was the sound of splashing. Her gaze followed the sound, and her mouth went dry with thirst and envy. She'd never seen a pool quite like this one. It was kidney-shaped, the lining giving the water a deep blue hue. When she spotted the source of the splashing, she stopped in her tracks, swallowing hard.

A lone feminine figure sat on the edge of the pool, her naked back to Janet. The woman leaned forward, letting the fingers of both hands slip through the water before she brought them to her face. She splashed some water over her shoulders, and Janet could practically see the droplets sizzle on her back.

Janet gulped again and glanced down at the name on the package. *Rebecca Thomas*. She licked dry lips, adjusted her sunglasses and cleared her throat.

"Excuse me. Mrs. Thomas?"

The woman jumped. Moving to cover her breasts, she glanced quickly over her shoulder and reached for the towel at her side.

"Sorry to bother you, Mrs. Thomas. But I have a special delivery package for you and I need a signature."

Rebecca was quickly on her feet, wrapping the towel around her body. She was smiling.

Janet stared hard at the woman who approached her, thankful for the sunglasses that hid the lust that she was sure would show in her eyes.

"Sorry to bother you," she repeated lamely, dropping her gaze. She began nervously juggling the package, clipboard and pen. "If you could just sign here." She held out the clipboard and pen, carefully averting her eyes.

Rebecca tilted her head to one side. "Janet O'Conner!"

"Huh?" Janet's head snapped back, eyes wide. The woman in front of her was smiling broadly, dimples creasing both cheeks.

"You don't remember me, do you?" She crossed her arms and pushed out her bottom lip, pouting. "I'm Becky Johnson."

Janet stared dumbly, her mind slow to respond. Then lightning struck. "Becky Johnson? *Little* Becky Johnson?"

Grinning, the woman nodded.

"I can't believe it's you. And I can't believe you recognized me." Janet was suddenly keenly aware of the sweat marks that she knew must cover her shirt.

"I haven't seen you since the sixth grade." Rebecca smiled again. "But I'd recognize that curly red hair anywhere. How are you, Janet?"

Janet managed to mumble a reply as her mind reeled back in time and she remembered who Becky had been nearly thirty years ago. Her heart thudded as she recalled the crush she'd had on Becky back then, when she was too young to know what all those emotions meant.

Becky was talking to her now, and Janet knew she was nodding and replying at all the right times. But she didn't have any idea what she was saying or what they were talking about. All she could think about was the searing pain in her ten-year-old heart when she'd watched Becky climb into the back of her family's station wagon to move away to a new neighborhood, a new school and a life that didn't include Janet.

Too late, Janet realized that Becky was staring at her, waiting for a reply.

"I'm sorry —" She shook her head.

"That's okay, I understand. But you will come back sometime? Maybe go for a swim with me?" She tilted her head to one side in the way that Janet now remembered clearly from their youth. "I'd love to catch up with you."

"Sure." Janet nodded, lying. Then Becky was leaning over the fence and signing her name by the X on the sheet of paper. Janet held out the package, making sure that their fingers didn't touch as she placed it in the other woman's hands. She stepped away. "Good to see you, Becky."

"You *will* come back, won't you, Janet?"

"I sure will," she replied, mindful of the perspiration marks beneath her arms. Embarrassed beyond belief, she traced her steps back to the truck and nearly jumped inside. She glanced quickly in the rearview mirror and groaned at the sight of the perspiration that clung to her forehead and matted her hair. "Yeah, right. As if I would ever come back to this house again. I don't think so." The last thing she needed was to have such strong memories and feelings reemerge. Even if she'd only been a kid back then, the memories were clear enough that she recognized them. The last thing she needed was to get emotionally involved with a married woman, and she knew that was exactly what would happen if they ever spent time together.

The truck's transmission protested as she slammed into reverse and backed out of the driveway.

For the next three days, Janet thought of little else but the brief encounter with her childhood crush. The more she remembered, the more curious she grew about the woman who had been out of her life for so long. It crossed her mind to stop by the house. She had been invited, after all. But her rational side convinced her that it was silly to pursue the fantasy she had conjured up. She knew all too well that the outcome would lead to nothing but disappointment.

On the fourth day, Janet felt a small smile when she saw another package addressed to Becky. She whistled happily throughout the day, purposely holding the package so that it would be her last delivery. Then she gave herself a good once-over in the mirror before turning on to Cottage Road and into Becky's driveway.

This time Becky was completely dressed in shorts and a T-shirt, and she welcomed Janet with an easy smile. They spoke briefly over the fence that surrounded the pool, and Janet found herself barely able to hold Becky's gaze while she shyly responded to Becky's subtle inquiries.

She left feeling giddy and silly and promising to return, all the while knowing that she never would. Not without an excuse, at least.

A week passed before another package arrived for Rebecca. This time Becky coaxed her inside the fence by offering her a glass of lemonade. Janet couldn't refuse. They sat together beneath a large beach umbrella, speaking only of the weather, the neighborhood, the ornamental shrubs that lined the fence.

The packages, all with a local P.O. box on the return address, began arriving every day, and Janet began looking forward to the last delivery of each day with eager anticipation. Each day she stayed at Becky's a bit longer than the day before, until their conversation grew easier and laughter flowed steadily.

Janet learned what Becky had done over the past thirty years. Apparently she had gone away to college in New York and gotten pregnant when she was barely twenty-one. She had married her husband reluctantly and stayed with him until their daughter went off to college. The very next day Becky filed for divorce and moved back to her hometown. She was just now starting over, and clearly relishing her freedom.

Janet began to open up too, telling Becky about Susan and their life together. Hesitant and unsure of

Becky's reaction, she'd been relieved when Becky didn't blink an eye.

Two weeks later the packages stopped. Janet couldn't believe it. The first day it happened, she went over and over her deliveries, distressed when she realized that there were none for Rebecca. The second day of no packages nearly sent her into a panic. She spent the entire day agonizing over whether or not to just drop by. She'd been invited. Many times. But she couldn't bring herself to do it. Especially once she recognized why she wanted to see Becky so badly. The old crush had come alive again, taking on a life of its own. But the crush of a forty-year-old woman was much different from that of a ten-year-old girl. And Janet decided that the best thing to do was to keep her distance.

Two more days passed without a delivery to Rebecca, and then it was the weekend. Janet thought she would go out of her mind.

She left for work early Monday morning, resolving to stop by Rebecca's even if she had nothing to deliver. But she lost her nerve and ended up returning to the office just before four o'clock. She hung around the garage and loading dock for a while, trying not to think about Becky, before finally heading to the parking lot. She slid behind the wheel of her car and was about to put the key in the ignition when she spotted Rebecca.

She was walking toward the customer service center, a small brown package in one hand. Janet sat still, waiting for her to reappear. Barely able to breathe, she couldn't help but wonder if maybe Becky was looking for her. But two minutes later Becky was emerging from the office and slipping sunglasses over her nose. Without looking around, she got inside her car and drove away.

Janet sat there, one thumb tapping the steering wheel as her thoughts ran in circles. Something was up, she was sure. She didn't know what it was, but she was going to try to find out. Before she could change her mind, she was back inside the office once again.

"Hey, Tom, what's up?" she called out.

"Hey, Janet. Why aren't you at home yet?" He was standing behind the counter, leaning against the conveyor belt that carried customers' packages to the loading dock.

"I'm on my way out now," she told him. "Just thought I'd stop and see if you need anything."

He raised an eyebrow suspiciously. "What do you want?"

Janet had to laugh. She wouldn't make a very good burglar. "Nothing, Tommy," she lied.

He eyed her for a moment. "Good. Then come back here and cover the counter for a minute. I need to visit the little boy's room."

Janet shrugged, not believing her good fortune. She waited until she was sure she was alone before scouring the packages piled up on the conveyer belt. It didn't take long for her to find what she was looking for.

There it was. The small package that Becky had carried in earlier. As she stared at the name and address on the box, it slowly dawned on her that this package was the exact size of the packages she'd been delivering to Becky.

"Well I'll be damned," she mumbled, unable to control the grin that tugged at the corners of her mouth.

The next day she pulled the truck into Rebecca's driveway, not a bit surprised to find Rebecca sitting under the umbrella, dressed in shorts and a T-shirt. A pitcher of lemonade and two glasses sat on a serving tray on the table. Janet took in the scene and started to smile.

"Hi," she called out. "Are you expecting company? Am I interrupting?"

Becky was on her feet, walking toward the gate with a smile. "No. You're not interrupting. Come on in."

Janet followed her, confidence high. "Are you expecting company?" she asked again.

"No, of course not. Why do you ask?"

Janet nodded toward the serving tray. "Two glasses." She thought she might have caught Becky blushing, but she wasn't sure.

Becky wrinkled her nose and put her hands on her hips. "Maybe I was hoping you'd stop by today."

"But I haven't been here in over a week." Janet watched the other woman squirm, delighting in the fact that she knew Becky's secret.

Becky chose not to respond, instead offering her a glass of lemonade. "I don't suppose you brought your suit today?"

Janet thought she detected a hint of sarcasm in

Becky's voice. Maybe it was closer to frustration. "Nope." She shook her head and raised a glass to her lips. "I can't stay. I've got a date."

Janet got the reaction she was looking for. Becky paled as she turned stunned eyes toward hers. "Someone special?" she asked.

"Very." Janet finished the lemonade in four quick swallows. She set the glass down on the table and licked her lips. "Thanks for the drink."

She noted Rebecca's frown and almost regretted her deception. Almost.

She stood up then and snapped her fingers. "Oops. I almost forgot to give you your special delivery." She took an overnight envelope from beneath her clipboard and placed it on the table.

Becky's brow furrowed. "But that's not —" She bit her lip.

"Not the package you were expecting?" Janet rocked back on her heels.

Becky slid her a look that Janet couldn't identify.

"Aren't you going to open it?" she asked. She cocked her head. "Now that I think of it, you never open your packages when I bring them."

Becky gauged her cautiously. "That's because I usually know what's in them."

Janet raised one eyebrow. "So what's in this one?" she asked, pointing to the overnight envelope.

"I'm not sure." Becky reached for the envelope and studied the handwriting. There was no return address. "Let's find out." She ripped it open and pulled out a smaller envelope. She eyed Janet briefly before slipping a finger under the flap of the envelope and extracting the card from inside.

"What is it?" Janet asked innocently.

"Looks like an invitation." Becky silently read the request on the card.

"From a secret admirer?" Janet was enjoying this too much.

"Something like that." Becky reread the card, realization dawning that the tables had definitely been turned. Janet felt triumphant. "So what time is your date tonight?" Becky asked coyly.

"Seven sharp." Janet grinned.

Becky tried unsuccessfully to hide a smile. "Uh-huh." She nodded. "And this date wouldn't be meeting you at the Rising Tide, would she?"

"Yep."

"Sounds romantic." Becky's eyes grew dark as she stared at Janet.

"I hope so." Janet swallowed hard under the heat of Becky's penetrating gaze.

"You better get going. You don't want to be late." Becky lifted her glass in a mock toast.

Janet smiled and backed away from the table. "See you later?" she asked.

"Yes, you will," was Becky's quiet reply.

Within a few moments, Janet was back at her truck. She slid open the door and looked at the brown package, then picked up the delivery note she'd already filled out and headed to the front door. Once there, she peeled back the sticker of the delivery note and placed it on the front door.

Attempts to deliver your special delivery package were unsuccessful. Sorry we missed you! Our driver will attempt to deliver your package tomorrow.

Janet stood back and read the note, a smile growing in her heart.

The Academy

Peggy J. Herring

Dakota liked walking the halls of the Academy when classes were in session. It gave her a sense of accomplishment to have things running smoothly. She had a good staff, and the faculty was excellent. As commandant, Dakota couldn't have asked for a more Academy-minded group working for her, and then to finally have Pastel here with her . . . it just didn't get any better than this.

As she rounded a corner of the east wing, Dakota entered the communications section. She could tell by the sudden drop in temperature that this particular period of instruction was nearly over. At any minute hundreds of female cadets would come pouring from classrooms and hurry to their next class, where the temperature would be more conducive to learning. Keeping straggling cadets moving through corridors in between classes had at one time been a challenge, but solving the traffic flow problem with cold-temperature therapy seemed to have taken care of things. A little discomfort went a long way in motivating the young.

Dakota remembered what it was like being a cadet here, and later in her career returning as a member of the faculty. Pastel had told her on many occasions that she'd fallen in love with her then.

"You were so regal and imposing the first time I saw you," Pastel had said. "You were lecturing on 'The Role of the Line Officer.' And you were so-o-o hot." She would always laugh then, and Dakota was never quite sure whether she was teasing her.

"Did you at least learn something?" Dakota remembered asking.

"Not that I recall. I was too busy fantasizing about you."

Dakota, of course, didn't remember Cadet Pastel. They didn't meet again officially until three years later when Lieutenant Pastel requested to be placed under Dakota's command days before their ship received orders for a deep-space mission. Dakota's biggest challenge then had been keeping morale in check; there was very little to do in deep space other than work, sleep, simulate recreation and make love. And with a completely new crew, it usually took several weeks before any coupling began. It had been a miserable time for everyone.

Lieutenant Pastel had always been an intriguing and illusive young officer, and her patience commendable. Dakota was drawn to such qualities and, in addition, liked Pastel's work ethic and her attention to detail. Pastel had let Dakota know in a low-key, subtle way that she was interested and available, but because of the difference in their rank she did nothing to further encourage her. Dakota, however, took her own role as commander of the ship quite seriously and chose not to pursue that avenue, but Pastel was always there, ready and waiting, and the loneliness and rigors of deep space eventually weakened Dakota's resistance.

Thank the goddess, she thought with a smile.

As she remembered all of that now, Dakota was amazed at how much time she had wasted back then. Falling in love with Pastel had taken her by surprise, and Dakota had spent a remarkable amount of time ignoring her own feelings. But Pastel had known she was winning and slowly chipped away at that thick layer of professionalism that threatened to keep them apart. They eventually became lovers, and Dakota realized after their first kiss that she had never really been in love before — this was an entirely new experience for her. Pastel pumped life back into her and gave Dakota things she never knew existed. In a way they had reversed roles, with the student suddenly becoming the teacher.

Less than two months later, Dakota and Pastel were transferred to different locations, and the shock of being separated was sobering. Pastel had been offered an executive officer position at a communications relay station, and Dakota had been promoted to Commandant of the Intergalactic Academy. These were considered once-in-a-lifetime positions that officers never refused.

So for eighteen months Dakota and Pastel had no contact with each other. Pastel's assignment placed her at a remote station where incoming communication was nearly impossible. And Dakota knew very well what remote assignments were famous for — they were worse than being sent out into deep space. The length of stay was longer and the practice of coupling very much a reality. The work was repetitive and boring there, but the overall mission of a relay station was vital to the fleet's overall mission and survival. Dakota was constantly reminded that Pastel was an attractive, desirable young woman, and their time together had been short. There were things Dakota hadn't said, things that she regretted *not* saying. And all the while that Pastel was working twelve-hour shifts and sleeping on a cot for eighteen months, Dakota was laying the groundwork for Pastel's next assignment.

And now she's here. Dakota grinned. *And once again my life is complete.*

The buzzer sounded as she came around another corner, and five seconds later cadets were everywhere. One of them saw Dakota and called the area to attention.

"As you were," Dakota said. "Carry on."

The temperature steadily dropped, and cadets scrambled to their next class. If nothing else,

Dakota's presence among them kept the noise level down in the hallway; usually the chatter was deafening. Now all she could hear was whispering and an occasional comment like "There's the commandant!" Or "Do we salute? When do we salute?"

Dakota smiled and greeted those who made eye contact. *Was I ever this young?* she wondered. Pastel was forever teasing her about the number of cadets who had a crush on her, but Dakota dismissed the idea as nonsense. She truly believed that cadets were too busy pursuing one another to give her another thought. She saw them as being terrified of her, which in a way was good. Dakota remembered feeling the same way about the commandant when she was a cadet.

"Some get into trouble just so you'll personally reprimand them," Pastel had said one morning as they dressed for work. "Your minions will do anything to get your attention." Then she added, "And that includes some members of the staff."

But Dakota had no time to think about such things. She had work to do and tried not to listen to Academy gossip. Most of it, however, couldn't be ignored, and some of it *did* involve her, but Dakota went on about her business without dwelling on the drama of it all.

She continued down another hallway and appreciated the temperature returning to normal. She entered the billeting unit where all doors were open and the individual cubicles were ready for inspection should she choose to do one. Dakota had her own philosophy about training. She believed in maintaining the proper military bearing and instilling a sense of honor in all cadets. Discipline was instrumental in producing good officers, and the technical aspects of a cadet's education were wasted if the fundamentals of military basics weren't achieved early on.

Dakota caught a glimpse of herself in the glass doors of the flight simulation chamber. *Regal and imposing,* she thought with a chuckle, remembering Pastel's comment. *Only someone who loves me would think so.*

She entered the chamber and glanced around. Flight simulation classes were held in the afternoon, so the chamber was supposed to be empty. But as Dakota slowly walked around she listened for any sounds out of the ordinary. At least sounds that were of a nature other than flight simulation. And before long she found what she'd come here for.

Dakota opened the door to the simulation control room and found two naked female cadets, their bodies in a tangled embrace, heaving and writhing — both well on their way to orgasm. Dakota cleared her throat and chose to look away. She began pacing as the shrieks of surprise and the scrambling for uniforms began.

"I want you both back in class immediately, and if anything like this ever happens again I'll see to it that disciplinary action is enforced. Do you understand?"

"Yes, Commandant. We were just —"

"I *know* what you were doing," Dakota said dryly,

"and there's a time and a place for you to do it. The time isn't now, and this certainly isn't the place." She continued her slow, steady pacing. "You've used poor judgment. You've chosen personal gratification over your training responsibilities. Those are not traits of a good officer. Now get dressed and get back to class."

Dakota left, shaking her head. It was the third time this month that she'd caught someone here. *You'd think they'd talk to each other and warn classmates where not to go.* Dredging up old Academy memories of her own, Dakota knew scores of places that cadets could go to be together. She and her first lover were pioneers in the art of making love in a utility closet, but it was always after-hours, when classes were over for the day. And those were precisely the places Dakota had been making her surprise visits. She didn't mind cadets' sexual activity. That was normal, healthy behavior. A fact of life at the Academy and anywhere else. What she took exception to was skipping class to do it. That showed a lack of discipline, and Dakota was a stickler for discipline.

She turned another corner and saw Pastel at the end of the hallway, opening the door to their cubicle.

"You're late," Pastel said.

"So are you, but I've got an excuse." Smiling, Dakota said, "I've been fishing."

Pastel laughed and pulled Dakota inside and sealed their door. "Catch anything?"

"Two in the flight simulation chamber."

"That's how many this month?" Pastel already had her hand inside the top of Dakota's uniform and kissed her cheek.

"Six," Dakota said. "How much time do you have?"

"An hour," Pastel said. "Kiss me, lover. We can talk later."

As Pastel's tongue danced in Dakota's mouth, it immediately made Dakota's knees weak. It was no secret at the Academy that they were lovers, but any type of open display of affection was discouraged. For Dakota and Pastel, their biggest challenge so far had been finding the time to be together. Their schedules were drastically different. With Pastel being one of the lowest-ranking members of the staff, her name came up regularly for all kinds of extra duty. Sleeping with the commandant gave her no special privileges.

"You like this?" Dakota whispered as she kissed Pastel's throat. She knew the answer already; she could feel Pastel trembling in her arms. "And this," she said as she kissed her deeply.

They eventually undressed and fell on the bed, their lips searching and hungrily finding each other again. Dakota loved the way Pastel surrendered to her. The way her blue eyes took on that dreamy, heavy-lidded look. The way her legs opened as an invitation. The way her passion was reflected in a murmur or sigh. Pastel was always first when they made love; it was better for them this way because Dakota took longer to arouse. They knew each other's bodies and were in tune from that first suggestive look until the last lingering kiss. It had been that way from the very beginning. They'd never experienced the awkwardness of new lovers.

Dakota was beside her and moved down her body as Pastel brought her knees up. Slow, deliberate kisses on Pastel's stomach and thighs made her tremble with anticipation all over again. Dakota knew what her lover wanted and how she wanted it. Long tenacious strokes of her flat tongue would bring Pastel around slowly, the way she liked it. Dakota took her time and savored each caress until Pastel began to moan.

Dakota loved this . . . loved the way Pastel lost control so easily and demanded even more from her. She would not be denied, and Dakota was always elated when Pastel's hands finally made their way to the back of Dakota's head and gripped her hair. It was wild and exciting and left them both wet and breathless, but this was just the beginning — a prelude to what was to come.

They were kissing again, and Pastel rolled on top of her. Dakota lived for this — having her this way, so totally connected and vibrant. She captured swaying breasts with her hands and mouth, teasing and licking Pastel's nipples until Pastel was delirious with pleasure. They were both ready now. As the rhythm continued and became more insistent with each grinding thrust, Dakota grabbed her and pulled Pastel closer. Heat raged between them, and Dakota was determined to give as much as she was getting.

Pastel collapsed on top of her, and Dakota took her in her arms and kissed her. Sweat coated their bodies as their ragged breathing slowly began to return to normal. Dakota outlined Pastel's earlobe with the tip of her tongue and nuzzled her neck.

"Where's the most interesting place you've ever made love here?" Dakota whispered. "At the Academy," she added, clarifying the question.

Pastel chuckled. "In the commandant's bed. What about you?"

Dakota laughed. "Good answer." She kissed Pastel again and was surprised at how quickly her body responded. "*Very* good answer."

No Experience Necessary
Saxon Bennett

I should have known when I answered the classified ad that it would bring trouble. It's like a job that offers to train you, no experience necessary, and then throws you into something you are totally unprepared to do. At first you panic, and then the intruding fingers of challenge, guided by ego, drives you to new and extreme heights. You tell yourself you can handle this and you learn everything on the fly. At the end of it you feel abused, less confident, yet extremely thankful, almost to the point of complete prostration, that you got out with your skin intact, barring a few

scars. After the experience you are like a shy teenager pulling down her first miniskirt; you don't know
whether you should let the guy stare or cross your
legs tighter so your virgin white panties don't show.
Then you hide your innocence and pretend the whole
thing never happened.

But that's how I met her. I answered the ad, intrigued, feeling a little dangerous and ripe for a
challenge. When she walked in the diner and sat
down at my table — knowing me from my description
of having a magenta mohawk and a tattoo on my
right wrist — I sensed that she was a woman who
knew what she wanted.

She knew what she was looking for, and, from the
moment I saw her, ego, challenge and risk begged for
her to take me anywhere she wanted to go. She was
slick, easing me into her situation with the briefest
explanation. No attachments, no past, no thought to
the future. She wanted pleasure . . . a lot of it.

"Have you ever lived in the present moment so
completely that nothing else mattered, Delores?" she
asked, looking me straight in the eye.

"Well, sure. I mean, isn't that like a really Zen
kind of thing?" I stammered.

"Yes, very Zen," she said, tapping the long
overdue ash from her cigarette with one fire-engine-
red fingernail.

I could feel her taking me in, sizing me up, and I
tried to see me through her eyes. I was a tomboy
butch, not quite a diesel dyke, more like a skate-
boarder chick that flirted with gender confusion. Was
I boy? Was I girl? I was girl/boy, or so that's what I
decided when I was fourteen. I have lived my life

that way ever since. So needless to say, most of the girls I dated let me pull the moves, put me in charge, made me feel the butch I never had the courage to be on my own. But this was different.

It wasn't like it started out weird. We did the normal things that constitute casual dating, nothing out of the ordinary, nothing the Pink Mafia would consider a sex foul. She had me over for dinner. I brought wine, two bottles, one red, one white. I didn't know what we were having. I toyed with the idea of flowers but figured she was the kind of woman who thought flowers were silly. I drove by the toy store and half considered edible panties, but good sense got ahold of me and said that might be pushing it. I refrained. She might not be that kind of gal either.

We talked about old girlfriends and therapy. We'd both been. It's almost a lesbian rite of passage. We compared therapists and their approaches. We talked about old girlfriends. That is, after all, how lesbians bond. Let's see how you got fucked over compared to how I got fucked over and then we can each figure out if the other one is trustworthy. We had one of those kind of dates. I felt safe when she walked me to my car and gently kissed me.

It wasn't until several dates later when we were lying in bed that she asked, "Ever think about trying anything different? Not that this isn't nice."

"Well, yeah," I said, rolling up on one elbow and putting a look on my face like I was prepared for extremes. I was sure the toy bag was about to miraculously appear on the bed. I'd been there before. The coy woman who starts out shy and demure and then gets you to tie her to the bed and strap on a wide variety of devices until you feel like the telephone man with his everpresent tool belt. Been there, done that, thought it was okay, maybe slightly overrated. But the toy bag didn't appear. I admit I breathed a sigh of relief because sometimes the toy thing made me feel more like a drill-press operator than a person, like it didn't matter that I was there just so long as an operator was on duty.

"Good," she said. "I like a woman with a sense of adventure."

She kissed me deeply and didn't show me the door until it was time for work the next day.

It was about then I thought I should be polite and invite her to my place, but she didn't seem interested. I mean, I know it's not a great place, but it did have its own peculiar charm. I tried not to be offended. She was, after all, taking me to the lesbian film festival. An evening full of lesbians watching lesbian movies full of lesbian sex. I was excited. She took me out to dinner, and then we cruised into the festival. She looked stunning in a short red dress and heels. I wore my vintage black suit. We looked the quintessential butch/femme couple. For once I didn't feel awkward. I felt like this was right. We made an entrance, and I liked it.

I sat down with my popcorn and waited for the lights to dim. She didn't look around, checking out the crowd like some of my dates, checking out the competition, looking for someone new or someone better. No, her eyes were on me. I felt special. I thought I might be falling in love. We hadn't talked

1

73**

about love, only about jiving in bed. She liked jiving
in bed.

The lights dimmed and the show began. I offered
her popcorn. She declined but sipped her soda and
put her hand on my knee. I settled in and got comfortable. I felt her hand creep up my leg in the
middle of the first short flick. I smiled into the
darkness. She cupped her hand on my cunt, moving
her finger along my clit. My eyes were glued to the
screen, but all I could think about was the way she
made me feel. How wet I was getting, surrounded by
intense woman-energy and watching sex on the movie
screen. She unzipped my pants and slipped her
fingers inside me. I lowered myself in the chair so
she could go deeper. I had one hand holding the
popcorn while my other hand gripped the chair arm
so I wouldn't make a sound as I came.

After the show she yanked me into the women's
rest room. We took a stall together. I was nervous
and tried not to show it. She stood up on the toilet
and lifted her skirt. She wasn't wearing any underwear. She pulled me toward her. I took her in my
mouth. She was wet. I licked her slowly and began to
finger-fuck her. Half of me was listening to the other
dykes in the bathroom talking about the flicks and
the other part of me was licking her like there was
no tomorrow.

I remember thinking this was kind of kinky, kind
of weird, but definitely a turn-on. So I was game. I
was hooked. I liked it. I knew it was dangerous to
feel that way, but I felt like the novice with all the
chips at the roulette table. I felt like I could win. I

had tasted the edge of paradise, and I couldn't back away now. I pulled up a chair and imagined the feast. I flicked out my napkin and grabbed a fork, pretending I knew what I was doing. She brought in the second course.

She called me at work. We didn't meet at her place anymore. We met out. She owned a cleaning business. She had the keys to half the city. She cooked me dinner at a French restaurant, some flaming gastronomical delight. I was impressed with her culinary skills. She was wearing a chef's hat and an apron, black heels and nothing else. She had a wild look in her eyes, and during dinner I tried to figure out the scenario. I've taken to doing that. I'm usually wrong. I'd almost lost track of the sex as I became obsessed with the motivation behind the scenario. Each date, each place, had its own theme. I was living in the theme park of eroticism.

It wasn't that the places and positions didn't turn me on. I was there. I was hot. It was incredible to have a woman so in tune with my body and so adept at manipulating its every nuance. And I was flattered that she devoted so much time to contriving these erotic evenings for our mutual pleasure. I wondered if she'd read them somewhere.

I began to read my own way through erotic literature. I caught the guy at the bookstore giving me looks as I set yet another stack up on the counter. It's a school project I told him. He rolled his eyes and rang me up. Perhaps I could get an advanced degree in erotic arts, Doctor of Fucktology, I thought as a threw *On Our Backs* and a variety of lesbian leather magazines on top of the stack. I

imagined myself wearing a well-tailored wool blazer
with leather patches on the elbows and pontificating
on the virtues of a sexual undertaking.

I was still dreaming of my academic career when
she led me to the stainless-steel table and bade me to
remove my clothes. Yes, we were having dinner in
the fancy French restaurant, but rather than dining
at a table we were eating each other. I felt my heart
quicken. I had grasped the scenario.

She put sliced tomatoes over my nipples, their
tips poking through the cored centers, a mushroom in
my navel, a carrot up my ass and a zucchini in my
cunt. I was the human salad. She spread Roquefort
dressing everywhere, and then she ate me. She
spread crêpes across her body, and I ate the main
course. We smothered each other with dessert. It was
gastronomical fucking. She kissed me good-bye and
the cleaning crew came in.

I lay in bed thinking about the evening, this one
and all the others. I fell asleep and dreamed I was
hanging on a meat hook and she pulled me toward
her and began to take me apart, dividing me into
pieces to be cooked up. I woke up in a sweat.

I thought about how we no longer met at her
place or mine. How sometimes we didn't really talk
except in the guttural language of fucking, of giving
and receiving, of finding and diving. How we left
each other trembling and sweat-covered without a
moment's whisper of tomorrow. I began to crave
tomorrow. Not the tomorrow of scenario, but rather
the tomorrow of I want you to meet my friends, go
to a party, hang out with me, act like a couple.

Instead, I lied to my friends. That's when you

know a love affair has gotten dangerous. You deny its existence. You tell tales about your whereabouts. I knew the signs. I'd been there before. It never turns out good; a boat off course seldom rights itself. This would turn out badly. How badly was up to me. But was I still a woman in command of her wits? I'd begun to wonder. I needed someone to snatch me from this place and deliver me not into temptation. I didn't figure Jesus Christ was going to show up any-time soon. I took her calls and did things I shouldn't have.

Until one day I was standing in the bookstore next to a petite woman in a yellow sundress. She looked like the Virgin Mary gone Delila. She looked at me tentatively. Suddenly, I felt like Don Giovanni, like I knew too much and would have given anything for innocence. She was shopping for lesbian fiction and seemed overwhelmed. I offered to help, thinking perhaps I could put my worldliness to good use. I picked out a few good books to start with, something to get a young lesbian on her way. For my reward she took me out for coffee.

Sitting across the table from this gorgeous baby dyke, I started to feel parts of my old self come back, like an old, dear friend who walks in just when you needed her most. I told Julie — that was the Virgin Mary's real name — all my best lesbian anecdotes, counseled her on her first lesbian love affair gone awry, handed her a napkin when she got weepy, and invited her out for dinner the next night. She hugged me tightly when she left, and I went shopping for a new vest to celebrate the occasion. Then I ordered flowers. Julie was the kind of girl that liked flowers.

The next night when she opened the door her face lit up and she made a big deal of finding a vase to put the flowers in. She kissed my cheek and blushed profusely. I immediately ascended to heaven. I felt shiny and new. She liked my vest and listened attentively when I told her about the new lesbian restaurant we were going to. She told me about how much she liked the first book she'd read. Don Giovanni had changed his chameleon coat and become Romeo, and that suited me.

I took her hand and we walked to the restaurant. My cell phone rang, and my heart dropped. I let it ring.

Julie looked over at me. "Aren't you going to answer it?" she asked.

I wavered for a moment. We walked past a big blue mailbox. "I don't think so," I said as I opened the lid and dumped the phone in it. It kept ringing in the bowels of the steel container.

Julie raised an eyebrow quizzically. "Why did you do that?".

"I'm sick of being so accessible," I replied.

She shrugged her slim shoulders. I opened the door to the restaurant. The place was packed, the food smelled good, my companion was perfectly darling and I knew I wasn't ordering the salad. Julie squeezed my hand excitedly. Tonight was going to be fun and *normal*. Suddenly, I craved normalcy like a lunatic cured finds incredible beauty in the daily life they once thought banal.

Later that night, as she slept in my arms and the moonlight danced lightly across her naked shoulders, I felt redeemed. She was worried that she wasn't experienced enough and apologized for her lack of knowledge. I almost told her no experience was necessary. I choked back the words, remembering another time, and murmured soft assurances instead.

"I like you just the way you are," I told her as I nestled between her soft breasts. She said I was sweet and guided my hand between her legs. I knew then that I need look no further for amorous adventures, that waking up next to a woman you can bring flowers to, take home and make uncomplicated love to was all the experience I would ever need.

Blueberry Clinic

Diana Tremain Braund

Dr. Sondra Ophelia Stearns moved the cursor about the text, moving several paragraphs from the bottom to the top. She rewrote the opening statement. She needed something high-powered and aggressive, something that would bite her audience. They had to walk away with the statistics and premise buried deep in their minds. She chewed on her bottom lip and stared at the title, "A Paradigm on Rural Teenage Mores: Today's Exploding Wanted Pregnancy and a View of the Social Crisis of the 21st Century."

As a public health physician in rural Jefferson

County, Maine, she had tracked a pattern of wanted pregnancies among young teen girls who coveted what they perceived as their mother's easy life of baby, welfare checks and more babies. She had presented a paper on the subject years before and now, as one of the leading experts, she had been asked to read a paper on the subject at the A.M.A. Convention in Albuquerque, New Mexico, the next day.

She and her colleague Meredith Clark, another physician at the Blueberry Clinic, would leave for Bangor in two hours. From there they would fly to Boston and then on to Albuquerque.

Meredith had gone home to do some last-minute packing. Sondra was already packed, and they had arranged for Meredith to pick her up at the office. She needed these precious few hours to complete some of the final editing, then she would change out of her scrubs and into her traveling clothes.

Sondra heard the familiar ding-dong of the bell that signaled someone's entrance into the reception area. She frowned at the clock. The Blueberry Clinic had closed at 2 p.m., the nurses were gone, and she had told the receptionist to lock up. Meredith wouldn't arrive for another thirty minutes.

Irritated, Sondra got up from her computer and stepped into the long hallway between her office and the reception area. She saw a woman with long red hair standing with her back to her.

Jamie Patterson waited in the reception area, her hands buried deep in the pockets of her jeans. She studied the diplomas on the wall. Sondra Ophelia Stearns, she thought, an unusual name for a Down East doctor, living in the heart of Maine's blueberry-

based economy. She also saw Meredith's diploma and
the seal from Harvard Medical School. She smiled as
she thought about the woman who not only was her
doctor, but one of her dearest friends.

"May I help you?"

"Yes, I have a small medical problem and I hoped
I could see my doctor." Jamie studied the tall slender
woman whose frame ended with a head of wavy black
hair. She liked her jaw, it was strong, the kind you
wanted to reach out and caress.

Sondra studied the other woman. "Our office
closed early because of a medical convention."

"I think it's something that needs to be looked at
tonight," Jamie persisted. "I don't think it will take
all that much time. Maybe just a quick exam and
then some kind of antibiotic. I have a sore throat,
and if I don't deal with it immediately it usually
turns into bronchitis."

"Have you ever been here before?"

"Yes, Meredith is my doctor."

Sondra walked over to long rows of files. "Your
name?"

"Jamie Patterson."

"While I am looking for your file, why don't you
step into the first treatment room on your left, and I
will be right with you."

"Sure," Jamie smiled provocatively.

Sondra walked over and locked the outside door,
she did not need any more interruptions tonight.
Then she entered the treatment area and softly
knocked on the door before entering.

Jamie was seated on the examining table, her
legs crossed at her ankles. Sondra noticed the curve

of her leg and the slim lines of her ankles. She adjusted her attention to Jamie's eyes.

"Let's look at that throat." She reached for a tongue depressor and adjusted the light.

Jamie licked her full lips and then opened her mouth.

"It isn't red or swollen." Sondra dropped the tongue depressor into the refuge can near the table.

Jamie reached over and stroked Sondra's arm. "You're kinda cute."

Sondra stepped back, flushed by the sudden intimacy.

"Thanks." She mumbled.

"In fact," Jamie slipped off the table and stepped within inches of the doctor. "You have the kind of lips that must be wonderful to kiss. I'd like to examine your throat with my tongue." She reached up and pulled Sondra to her.

Sondra did not resist, but this was madness, she thought. She had never done anything like this before in her clinic. She felt Jamie's tongue dance around her own and marveled at the woman's sweet taste. She reached down and pulled Jamie's hips tight against hers, and she could feel her own blood pressure rising.

She stroked Jamie's hips with the palms of her hands and sensed the burning heat of Jamie's skin underneath her clothes.

Jamie's hands pulled Sondra hard against her, their breasts rubbing against each other. She pushed her hand down the back of Sondra's green scrubs.

"I've got to have you," she said explosively as she

pushed Sondra back onto the examining table. "I've got to have you, now."

She pulled the tie on the front of Sondra's scrubs and eased the pants down over Sondra's hips. She caught her breath at the first sight of the black triangle that seemed to pulsate against Sondra's white underpants.

"I can't. Not here." Sondra gripped the edges of the examining table. For a brief second she questioned whether she had locked the front door. But in the heat and swirl of passion, she found she didn't care.

"Where else but here?" Jamie said provocatively.

Jamie hooked her finger in the edge of Sondra's undies and began to stroke the edge of her passion. She could feel the heat as it tingled on her fingertips. She bent over her and licked Sondra's stomach and felt the woman suck in her air and hold it.

"Don't stop now," Sondra said between clenched teeth.

"I don't intend to," Jamie said as her tongue licked up inside Sondra's smoldering thighs. Then as her fingers held the undies slightly to the side, she let her tongue dance around the same spots she had touched with her fingers just moments before.

"Oh yes," Sondra gasped.

Using both hands Jamie slipped Sondra's panties off and her tongue began to feast on a passion that seemed to shake the very floor she was standing on. As she felt the first stirrings of Sondra's climax, she slipped two fingers into Sondra's heated womanliness.

Panting and gasping for air, Sondra reached down

and pulled Jamie on top of her, careful not to dislodge the fingers that were now pushing her to new heights of passion. She gripped Jamie's face in her hands and pulled her mouth to hers. She had to taste their pleasure.

Sondra's fingers dug into Jamie's back as yet another orgasm pulled at her soul.

Jamie slipped another finger inside of Sondra and teased her yet to new heights. She felt yet another wave of passion tug at her, and she knew she did not want this to end.

Sondra exploded and Jamie felt a rush of hot liquid spread over her fingers.

As Sondra lay back gasping, Jamie kissed her neck and then the jaw she loved to touch. Sondra pulled Jamie's lips to hers in a meaningful kiss. She stroked the long red hair that felt like crushed satin.

"What a wonderful surprise," Sondra said between gasps.

"Uhmmmm. I thought so." Jamie rested her head on Sondra's shoulder.

Sondra chuckled.

Jamie raised her head and looked at the doctor. "Why the chuckle?"

"You've given new meaning to the term emergency medical examination. I was wondering what you were up to. But I shouldn't be surprised. Over the years, we've made love in some pretty weird places. Professor Smith's lecture hall at the university. In the water at Hadley's Lake. What's next? The airplane?"

Jamie gave Sondra a half-smile. "Maybe."

Sondra frowned. "We made love last night, this morning. Not enough?"

Jamie kissed her long-time lover. "I just wanted to give you something to think about on that long trip to Albuquerque. I am going to miss you, darling."

"I love you. I want to make love to you." Sondra said softly.

Jamie looked up at the clock. "Meredith is going to be here in another five minutes."

"How did you know?"

Jamie grinned sheepishly. "Because I called her and told her to not be early for once in her life. She seemed to understand. Besides," Jamie said as she eased herself off her lover and held out her hand to help Sondra up, "I want you to look forward to coming home."

Sondra pulled her lover to her, and they stood encircled in each others arms. "I love you, Jamie Patterson. Ten years and never a dull moment." She kissed Jamie on the nose. "And I promise you another ten years and guaranteed not a dull moment."

They both heard the *ding-dong* as the door to the reception room opened. "That's Meredith," Sondra frowned.

"Go get dressed." Jamie kissed her lover again. "I'll go visit with our friend."

The Garden
Christine Cassidy

Caroline looked out through the screen at her window boxes. Too late. The sun had edged south around the big building facing 19th Street and was already illuminating the white petunias and sickly red geraniums. She'd have to wait until after sundown to water them. She took a sip of lukewarm milky coffee and threaded her way back to her old green chair, where she continued to stare out the window.

What was it Ed had said? "What is the story? What is your vision?"

Hard to believe she wouldn't be here anymore,

living in the city she loved more than life itself. How would she keep her ass in shape if she wasn't going to be climbing five flights of stairs anymore? Not that climbing the stairs had kept her from gaining anyway — a few pounds here, a few pounds there. Over the years she'd put on more weight than she liked to admit. That Ann loved her despite the extra pounds amazed her.

She glanced across the courtyard to the rooftops of the apartments on 19th Street. The Buddhist was in his garden again. After having changed from his early-morning robe, he was wearing shorts and a T-shirt, bending over his own flowerpots and deadheading cherry-topped geraniums that seemed never to die.

Ed said, "You have to remember to keep your personal lives separate from your business life."

Caroline laughed silently. The pornographer and the poet, going into business together. Buying a business, no less. An *existing* business, everyone said sagely. Not some new media startup with a big IPO in the wings, they implied. In other words, they'd have the money only through hard work, not via the courtesy — Caroline thought of it as the kindness of strangers — and risk-taking dollars of money-grubbing, thestreet.com-watching Wall Street twenty-somethings. Hah. What did any of them know? She and Ann would buy the magazine company and move to New Jersey. All their years of experience in the business would make them, eventually, comfortable. It wasn't like they would be publishing craft magazines old women bought at the newsstand and subscribed to through Publishers Clearinghouse.

Was this it, then? Was this what age brought? The road not taken? Other roads magically appear and there you go? Just like that?

There was a box of blueberries on the white marble coffee table. Ann had bought them at the A&P on Eighth Avenue that morning. Maybe she would buy some cream this afternoon at the deli and serve them up to Ann in bed later this afternoon. How long had it been?

She went into the bedroom and watched Ann sleep. Her face was like gesso, an unlined palette to write herself on. Caroline touched her leg and Ann stirred, still deep in sleep, an early-afternoon nap, the bedclothes rumpled around her. She ached for Ann's touch.

Who would they be in New Jersey? Old married lesbians buying their first home in a subdivision? Voting on whether to raise school taxes, shopping at the Home Depot, suburban. Caroline shuddered at the thought of it. But there she'd have a real garden, a garden as good as the Buddhist's on 19th Street. She'd have a freezer with a real door.

"You'll be a professional lesbian," Ann had said to her the night before as Caroline sat inexplicably crying on the pink couch.

"I just feel something's happened to Margaret," she said, the pain in her chest nearly unbearable. "Something's happened to her. She's sick, you know. Anything could have happened."

Ann nodded. "Margaret's a professional lesbian."

Cryptic, but the meaning wasn't lost on her. "I wouldn't be here without Margaret," she said. "I don't exist without Margaret."

Margaret was a long-time supporter of the magazine they wanted to buy. She was an exquisite essayist, had published pieces in *The New Yorker*, *Harper's* and Salon.com. Caroline had had the honor to meet her once, at a panel at a gay writers' conference, through Leslie, her friend who also wrote poetry. They'd bumped into each other several times since. Leslie had once been Margaret's lover, and Margaret wrote a lovely little story about a threesome that involved the butch Leslie.

Yesterday afternoon, Caroline, not knowing why, reread the threesome piece in a years-old anthology she plucked off her bookshelf. It was then Caroline began to cry. When Ann got home, she found her on the pink couch, drinking a vodka, still crying, and Ann suggested she was afraid of being a "professional lesbian," meaning a lesbian who would meet the world with full force, totally out. Everyone would know. It wouldn't matter that when people met her, she'd be dressed in suburban garb, a tea-length cotton dress, with sandals and a matching purse.

Last night Caroline dreamed someone stole the new air conditioner. There was a gaping hole in the window. Her petunias and sick geraniums were upended on the fire escape.

Ann dreamed she was lost in San Francisco, her true hometown. Her left front wheel had gone off the road, and she'd been using her wipers, thinking they would wipe away the fog.

In the morning, watching the Buddhist, robed and spiritual-looking, attend to his daily rooftop devotions, Caroline thought maybe her crying wasn't about Margaret at all, just like Ann said.

She kissed Ann's cheek, watching her nap. It was warm. The sun was shining through the window, and the flowers looked almost healthy.

"You may not know exactly *which* road you're on, but you've got to take the steps, you've got to be ready."

Ready for what? To move right out to New Jersey and buy a home? To register to vote in a subdivision? To buy a car?

"Ed's right, you know," Ann had said later. "We've got to be ready to jump right in, go take over the business."

Caroline's cheeks burned. Was she so myopic that she couldn't even see the big picture, the real story? Of course it wasn't about voting and shopping at the Home Depot on a brilliant Saturday morning with the rest of the home-repair crowd.

She trailed her fingers down Ann's naked back, feeling the ribs there, her spine, the vulnerable place where the white shorts met her waist. She slid a finger underneath the elastic. This lean, cougar-like body was hers. How was it possible? How did she deserve this kindness that oozed from her pores even in sleep?

She kissed the naked thigh just below the shorts. She trailed up under, her tongue a serpent. Ann mewled in response. She hadn't failed, after all.

That night she watered the plants and said, "There are lots of professional lesbians. I'll just be one more."

Ann smiled, her sky-blue eyes still dreamy from the afternoon. "Will you, now?"

"Yes, just like Margaret. Just one more in a big

pool of lesbians, professional lesbians. What does it really mean anyway? That I can talk to the press? So what." She lifted her jaw, almost in defiance, imagining her parents, her grandparents, the little ones her siblings had put out, all standing in a circle at the next family reunion staring at her. *There's a professional lesbian*. Hah! "Let's add a horoscope to the magazine."

Ann looked at her. "Okay."

"But not too general. More specific. A good one that they'll want to read. They'll buy it just for the horoscope."

She knew that wasn't why the young lesbians would subscribe to the magazine. They'd buy it because she and Ann would be the new publishers, because the magazine was already good and true to their lives. Maybe some of them knew that Ann wrote a very successful pornographic series for another lesbian publisher; Ann was already a professional lesbian. Once, when they were sitting in a favorite restaurant on Seventh Avenue, tourists approached her and asked if she were *the* Ann Lombard, the writer. Caroline had been proud.

"The morning glories are sad," she said. Ann sipped her scotch and watched her. "The cable guys lied. They said they were only going to fix the cables on the front of the building." One cable wire was completely missing, and now the wilted end of a once-climbing vine was pathetically draped over the fire escape ladder to the roof. Caroline looked down to the second-floor roof where Jeremy and Peter always grew their own morning glories and let them curl up the cable wire toward her window where they bloomed. Every summer, there they were, blue as Ann's eyes, right next to the bedroom window. "I'm glad I called Leslie to see if she could find out about Margaret, to see if she's okay."

"Come here." Ann slipped up behind her and held her. "Margaret's okay. The morning glories will be fine. Ditto the geraniums." Ann kissed her neck.

If they moved in the fall, what would happen to the plants? Who would take care of them? Maybe she could give them to Ed. She suddenly imagined having a full-sized refrigerator, with a real freezer. Inside the freezer, she'd stack plastic tubs of homemade pesto. She'd take the pot of basil with her, the thyme and rosemary too. Sin to waste. And new clay pots were expensive, even in New Jersey, even at the Home Depot, or so she'd heard.

"Promise?" She turned and looked Ann in the eye, daring and hoping.

"Promise."

Long Ride Home
Kate Calloway

I was milking the last bit of August sunlight, not wanting to go inside yet. The garden still needed me, or maybe it was I who needed the garden. Either way, the hard work was a welcome diversion. I'd been in the small Oregon town just long enough to learn where things were, but not quite long enough to meet anyone. I'd spent my time pouring what little money I had into a fixer-upper along the McKenzie River. I loved the place. The master bedroom looked out over the winding river through west-facing windows, and the rooms, far more than I needed, were large and inviting. Sure, the roof leaked and the closets smelled musty. Yes, the grounds were overgrown. But, hell, I'd gotten the place for a song and it was everything I'd ever dreamed of, even if it was too big for one woman and a cat.

Outside, the air was starting to cool and to the west the sky was showing off its hues of tangerine and aqua. My hands were caked with dirt but I wiped my forehead with the back of my hand, knowing it was already streaked with the loamy Oregon soil where I'd wiped away the sweat earlier. Sophie, my Abyssinian, had long since tired of all the hoeing and weeding and was curled up on a throw rug in the open doorway, catching the day's final rays of warmth. When the phone rang in the living room, the sound startled us both.

"You get it," I said. "Tell whoever it is I'm not interested." Sophie responded to this about the way I figured she would. She yawned, hiked her rear leg up past her ear so she could better reach her nether regions and settled in for some serious grooming.

Sighing, I leaned the hoe against the fence, brushed my hands on my dirt-stained sweatpants and headed in to see who was leaving a message.

"Honey, it's Mom. Pick up. I have bad news."

My mind reeled. Had something happened to one of my grandparents? Was it Dad? I grabbed the phone, trying not to smudge the receiver with dirt.

"What's wrong?" I asked.

"Oh, there you are. I thought I was going to have to talk to that machine again. I do wish you'd try harder to reach the phone. Or set it for more rings.

It makes me feel like you're screening your calls, deciding whether or not to pick up."

"Mom, what bad news? You made it sound like an emergency." Already I was regretting having picked up. This was probably just her way of hooking my interest until she got around to what she really wanted to talk about. I carried the phone into the kitchen, cradled the receiver under my chin and started working on my hands.

"Remember Ellie Lane? The girl who ended up in that mental institution? Well, of course you do. What a silly question." She giggled, like someone who'd just remembered a naughty joke. Just that fast, my heart thudded and I turned off the tap. Talk about a name from the past! I hadn't thought of Ellie in ages. I was surprised my mother could mention her name so coolly. Had she forgotten? I knew my mother was the master of compartmentalization, but could she have actually forgotten about Ellie? I leaned against the sink and lowered my voice to what I hoped sounded calm and collected.

"Something happened to Ellie Lane?" Mild interest. Idle curiosity.

"Oh no, dear. Not her. Her parents. You remember Ned and Stella Lane? He ran for mayor last year. Anyway, they were killed in a car wreck this week. Right outside of town heading down Bear Mountain. Apparently one of those big rigs jackknifed and the Lanes' car, one of those teeny Miatas, skidded right underneath it. Dreadful accident. It's been all over the news here."

It would be. Even back then, Ellie's father had

been on the city council. Suddenly I could picture him, though I'd only seen him once. Tall and dark, like Ellie, with the same penetrating eyes the color of maple syrup. Hers were warm and liquid, with pupils so big they melted into the irises when she smiled. But his, as I remembered, raged with anger.

"Honey, did you hear me? Are you there?"

"Yeah, I'm here, Mom. That's really sad." I couldn't for the life of me figure out why she was telling me this. The last time she'd uttered Ellie's name, it had been with disgust. "You are never, ever to mention that girl's name in this house," she'd said. And I never had. Now, years later, she acted like it had never happened. Was my mom starting to lose it? I furrowed my forehead, trying to remember the night it happened. It was still the same blur it always had been. The only part I could remember with clarity was my mother's anger.

"I wasn't going to tell you at all, except I seem to remember you and Ellie were school chums once, and I thought that with its being summer vacation, you might want to come back for the services."

School chums? Had she really managed to box what had happened into something as manageable as *school chums*? My heart raced. It was as if a thick and heavy fog were being lifted, as if someone were tugging at a burlap sack draped over my head. Apparently my silence was mistaken for acquiescence.

"The weather's lovely right now. And your classes don't start for quite a few weeks now, right?"

She knew that fall classes didn't start at the community college until the second week in September.

My mother knew my calendar better than I did. I could practically hear her brain humming, working out the math. If she could get me back to Idaho, she might be able to keep me for several weeks.

"I doubt Ellie Lane even remembers me," I said, feeling my cheeks warm. No sooner had I said it than I realized it was a lie. Suddenly I knew Ellie would remember me, although I wasn't entirely sure why. "How's Dad?" I asked, changing the subject.

"Oh, you know. Works too hard, rests too little. I wish I could get him to go out once in a while. They've opened up a darling theater downtown. Maybe you and I could go. It was his idea, by the way."

I waited, hoping she'd elaborate. "What was?" I finally asked. My mother had always done this — change subjects midstream, yanking me from one topic to another.

"Coming back home. He's the one who thought you might want to, you know, pay your respects. I told him it was nonsense, but you know how your father is. Once he gets an idea in his head, he won't let go of it. I think he really just wants to see you, Bean. He misses you."

She had to throw that old "Bean" in. She saved that up for special moments, when she thought she needed an extra punch. "Bean" packed an emotional wallop and she knew it.

"Well, I've got a lot going on here," I said, searching the fridge for something stronger than light beer. I found a Carta Blanca in the back and took a long swallow.

"How hard can it be to get ready to play basketball? I mean, it's not like you have to prepare lesson plans."

"I don't play basketball, Mom. I coach. Anyway, I didn't mean work, exactly."

"You've met someone?" The hope in her voice pained me. Briefly, I considered lying. I'd done it all through college — made up stories of phantom dates just to placate her. I shook my head, suddenly not willing to play that game. If she was embarrassed to have an unmarried daughter, that was her problem.

"Sorry, Mom. No such luck."

The silence on the other end told me I'd hurt her. I could picture her pursed lips and knew she was mentally adding up my offenses. I'd turned my back on a perfectly respectable career opportunity teaching literature at Idaho State to coach basketball in this podunk junior college in Oregon. I'd wasted all that time and money on college and hadn't even landed a husband. To add insult to injury, I didn't come home often enough. My mother's dreams were being dashed one by one. She'd tried so hard to teach me the finer points of etiquette. She'd made sure I had a strong background in the arts. Throughout my childhood, she'd sacrificed her own wardrobe to make sure mine was worthy of the boys on the west side of town whose fathers were lawyers and doctors. She'd envisioned a time when I'd marry one, and we'd all move over to live among the rich and cultured class. Knowing I was such a huge disappointment to her had always made me feel bad. I took another drink of the beer and waited for her to break the silence.

"Well, I just thought you'd want to know. I promised your father I'd mention it. Maybe, when

you're not too busy, you can give him a call, Bean."
Guilt worked its way across the phone line as I
listened to my mother hang up. Then, with a
vehemence that was both unexpected and unsettling,
I slammed down my receiver, causing Sophie to bolt
for cover.

I marched through the house, turning on lights,
surprised at my anger. My insides churned and my
face felt flushed and I wasn't entirely sure why. This
wasn't the first time my mother had tried to manipu-
late me into coming home. And I knew how she felt
about my coaching job. So why was I so angry?
Sophie tentatively followed me into the bathroom and
jumped up on the sink counter, watching me disrobe.

"You know what ticks me off?" I asked, throwing
my clothes on the floor.

Sophie regarded me with infinite patience.

"That after all this time, out of the blue, she
brings up Ellie Lane like nothing ever happened. Like
she doesn't remember forbidding me to ever mention
Ellie's name in the house! That's what ticks me off!"
I realized I was shouting and reached down to stroke
Sophie's head. "Don't worry, Soph. It was a long time
ago. Way before your time." Suddenly, a chill ran
right through me.

I wheeled around and turned on the hot-water
faucet, more for something to do than anything else.
My mind refused to focus, though it was suddenly
flooded with images it hadn't allowed to surface in
years. Slowly, I sank down into the nearly scalding
water and made myself remember.

* * * * *

Number Nine was actually taller than I was. That was the first thing I noticed, stepping onto the court. West High, our crosstown rivals, wore yellow and white uniforms, which seemed to accentuate her dark good looks. She'd have stood out anyway, though. Right away, I knew she could play. I was the tallest player on my team and was used to outjumping my opponents for the ball, but on the first play of the game, Number Nine not only outjumped me, but after slapping the ball to a teammate, she raced downcourt, caught the ball on the fly, took three graceful bounds toward the net and swooped in for an easy layup. Then, in a moment I had never forgotten, she turned back, locked her gaze on me and smiled radiantly.

From that point on in the game, we were inseparable. I'd never worked so hard or played so well in my life. It was one of those nights when I couldn't miss. Every ball I threw toward the basket dropped in. But every time I turned around, Number Nine had her hands in my face, blocking my path. We dogged each other, maneuvering for position, pushing ourselves beyond our limits.

My best shot of the night came with less than a minute to go in the fourth quarter. I stole the ball from West High's forward, dribbled right past an amazed Number Nine, drove toward the net and, stopping six feet from it, sank a jumpshot that put us up by one. I was physically ready to drop but mentally pumped. I wanted this game. For some reason, getting the best of Number Nine had become my sole obsession.

West High threw the ball in to her, and she immediately raced downcourt with me right on her heels. She stopped at the top of the key as if to shoot, but I blocked her shot. She feigned left, a move I anticipated, which seemed to frustrate her. She pivoted to the right and again I was in her way. Our eyes locked, and despite the fact that I was winded and sweating, I grinned.

It was as if time stopped completely, though both of us could hear the crowd counting down the final seconds. Then, surprising me, she took one step back, raised the ball over her head as if to pass it away and lobbed a perfectly rotating ball toward the net. The whole gymnasium seemed to hold its collective breath. In what seemed like slow motion, I turned my head and watched in absolute awe as the orange ball slipped through the net without a whisper.

On away games, it was customary for the girls' team to stay after the game to cheer on the more important boys' team before riding home together on the bus. I showered and changed into my street clothes, dawdling longer than necessary in the locker room. I wasn't sure why, but I wasn't really eager to join my teammates up in the bleachers, despite their assurances that I'd played a good game. It wasn't so much the way the game had ended, I thought, but more that the game had had to end at all. Mulling this over, I made my way out of the locker room and headed toward the gym.

"Good game," a voice said, making me stop in my tracks. I wheeled around and found Number Nine

grinning at me. She was even more striking out of
uniform. She wore faded Levi's and a white-ribbed
muscle shirt that showed off more than just her
tanned muscles. I noticed she wasn't wearing a bra
and caught myself blushing. Her short hair, still wet
from the shower, was brushed back from her forehead, but one dark tendril fell loose in a curl above
her eyebrow. She wore a gold stud in each earlobe,
her one concession to jewelry. Like me, she wore no
makeup.

"Yeah, well. You did all right yourself," I said, embarrassed to be staring. Ellie threw back her head
and graced me with a full-throated laugh.

"That was the luckiest damn shot I ever made in
my life. You had me penned in. Honest. You played a
great game. Ellie Lane." She extended a firm, warm
hand and we shook.

"Jean Bailey," I said, noticing for the first time
how her eyes seemed to pool like honey.

"Oh. *Jean.* I thought they were calling you *Bean.*"

"Uh, well, yeah, they were, actually. It's a nick-
name."

"As in string bean? Cause you're tall and thin?"

"Something like that," I said, suddenly embarrassed again. "My dad started it, I guess. It just sort
of stuck."

"I like it," she stated. "Bean. I like that."

We were walking toward the gym, neither of us in
a hurry. The cool night air was refreshing after the
heat of the gym. I noticed goose bumps on Ellie's
arms, but she didn't seem to mind.

"You know what else I like about you?" she said, making me stop again.

"No. What?" She didn't even know me. How could she like something about me?

"I like that you don't slouch. So many tall girls, they try to hide the fact they're tall. But you walk like you don't care if you're taller than boys or not. You want to go get a Coke?"

"Uh, we're supposed to watch the guys' game, then ride home on the bus."

"So, we'll be back before halftime. Or if you want, I could give you a ride home." She saw me hesitate and shrugged. Suddenly, she was the one who seemed embarrassed. "That's okay, then. Anyway, it was nice meeting you."

"Hang on a second," I said. "I just have to let the coach know." Before I could stop myself, I was dashing headlong for the gym.

Ellie drove a cherry-red '66 Mustang with dual exhaust pipes that sounded like she'd intentionally removed the muffler. She drove with her left hand on the wheel, while her right hand worked the radio buttons.

"You like Motown?"

"I guess so. Actually, I'm kind of limited, music-wise. My mother refuses to let me listen to anything but classical. She's afraid rock will stunt my growth or something."

"You're kidding!" She looked at me sideways. "You're not." She was trying to suppress a smile.

"What's so funny?"

"Well, *look* at you! Just how tall does she want you to get?" I had to admit it was kind of funny, and I found myself laughing with her. "Come on. I'm going to convert you."

"Where are we going?"

"To the best Motown collection in town." Without another word, she rolled down the window to let in the cool night air, turned up the volume on the radio and stepped on the accelerator.

"They won't be home for hours," she explained, pulling into the driveway of a three-story estate. I followed her into the house, staring open-mouthed at the grandeur. "This is my mom's night at the historical society and my father's night at the Elk's." She led me past the huge, plushly appointed living room toward a palatial kitchen. I was trying not to gawk, but Ellie Lane lived in a mansion. "You like rum and Coke?" she asked, stopping at a leather-and-glass wet bar. When she saw the look on my face, she laughed. "I know, I know. You've never tried it. Afraid it'll stunt your growth."

It was hard to resist her quirky logic, and besides, it felt like a good night for firsts. I watched her grab bottles, an ice bucket and glasses, then followed her up wide carpeted stairs to her room.

"So, you're rich," I said matter-of-factly, openly admiring her room. The size of a small apartment, it was covered from floor to ceiling with posters of everything from black musicians to Georgia O'Keeffe prints. Ellie handed me a drink and shrugged.

"Eclectic taste, huh?"

I knew what *eclectic* meant, but it was the first time I'd ever heard a girl my age use the word in conversation. Then again, Ellie was turning out to be unlike any girl I'd ever met.

"Okay, we're going to start with the Temptations." She leaned over an impressive stereo system, delicately pulled a vinyl record from its jacket and lovingly placed it on the turntable. In a few seconds the room exploded with sound, and I looked around in amazement. Speakers, suspended from the ceiling, circled the room, creating a surround-sound stereo effect that practically shook the walls. "Come on!" she said, taking a gulp of her drink. You can't listen to this stuff sitting down. You gotta move, girl." She jumped up and started swaying to the beat. Her eyes were closed and I watched her for a minute, in awe of her supple grace. Then, taking another gulp of the rum and Coke for strength, I stood up and joined her.

We talked, of course, and laughed and drank, but mostly Ellie and I just danced. She had a good voice and sang along huskily from time to time. The music poured through me, the strong rhythmic cadence touching places Bach and Beethoven had never reached. I found I liked dancing and felt myself let go, unafraid to have Ellie see me "getting down," as she put it. When the music switched to a slow song, it wasn't strange at all to feel Ellie take me in her arms and pull me against her. My eyes were closed, and though I felt a little lightheaded from the rum, I didn't pull away when her hands began caressing my back.

"You move good," she said, whispering against my cheek.

"So do you," I whispered back, surprised at the huskiness of my voice. The rum had worked its way to my extremities, and parts of me tingled. I had never felt so light on my feet, so alive. I felt Ellie's fingers push my hair off my shoulder, felt her warm breath against my neck. A shiver ran down my spine, and new parts of me tingled.

"Is this okay?" she asked, moving her hand so that her fingers lightly traced my breast. I felt myself start to gasp, but before I could utter a protest, Ellie's lips were on mine. They were soft yet insistent, and I found myself opening to her.

Delicious waves of pleasure rolled over me as Ellie and I discovered the magic of kissing. Our lips fit together as if they were made for this very purpose. Our bodies pressed against each other, bringing exquisite torture to each place we touched. The music changed, but neither of us pulled away.

I felt Ellie slide her hand inside my shirt, her lips never leaving mine, as she unhooked my bra. Gasping, I felt myself tremble as my shirt fell to the floor and, for the first time in what seemed like hours, Ellie's lips left mine.

My whole body shuddered and my knees gave way as Ellie knelt before me, moving her mouth across my breasts, devouring first one nipple, then the other. I found myself falling and felt Ellie's hands guide me to the floor. She was on top of me then, and our mouths found each other, found a new rhythm that was more urgent, matching the beat of Marvin Gaye, the beat that Ellie's hips were making against mine as her hand slid down between my legs, making me cry out.

Suddenly, the door banged open, flooding the darkened room with furious light. Ellie rolled off of me, leaving my bare breasts exposed to the horror-stricken stare of Mr. Lane. Silently, he strode across the room, dragged the needle in a hideous screech across the record and turned off the music. The ensuing silence was deafening. Ellie stood motionless as I fumbled for my shirt. I watched as Ellie's father took the stack of records and, one by one, snapped them in two over his knee. Ellie was speechless.

"Mr. Lane. Don't, please. It was all my fault," I whispered, my voice raspy with fear. He held one last record aloft but stopped to look at me, his black eyes searing me with hatred.

"Go get in the car. Mrs. Lane and I will drive you home."

I looked at Ellie, helpless with fear and mortification. Ellie's face had gone beet red, but she continued to stare at her father, who refused to even glance in her direction.

"Dad," she said.

"Don't you ever call me that again!" he hissed. In two strides, he crossed the room and backhanded Ellie so hard she hit the wall and fell against the bed. Then he turned to me and, in a voice so cold it made me shiver, he repeated the order, "Go get in the car."

Mr. and Mrs. Lane never spoke a word in the car,

except to get my name and address. I mumbled quiet directions from the back seat, but neither of them uttered another word the whole way home. Mr. Lane accompanied me to our front door and insisted on ringing the doorbell.

"It was my fault," I repeated, but my voice was barely audible even to me. When my mother opened the door, her face went white.

"Mrs. Bailey? Ned Lane." He introduced himself like he was running for office.

My mother looked from him to me, clearly at a complete loss. I could tell she recognized the name and was impressed that a city councilman was on her doorstep. But I knew she couldn't fathom what I had to do with it.

"May I speak to you privately?" he said. His words were solicitous, but I could still hear the venom in his voice. I edged past my mother and slipped into the house, straining to hear his words. He spoke in such controlled, clipped tones, I could only catch phrases: ". . . engaged in unhealthy practices . . . daugh- ter's a sick girl . . . back to the hospital . . . keep an eye on yours . . . hopefully a phase . . ."

"What's wrong, Bean?" My father's voice startled me so badly I jumped. Then, blood pounding in my head, I turned and ran straight for the bathroom, slammed the door and proceeded to get violently ill.

Sometime later my mother came into the bath-room and stood with her hands on her hips watching me heave over the porcelain bowl. When at last I was able to stand, there were tears streaming down my face.

"Well, I hope *that's* out of your system. You are

never, ever to mention that girl's name in this house. Is that understood?"

Dumbly, I nodded, unable to stop shaking.

"Alcohol makes people do ridiculous things. It's best just to put this behind us now. We'll forget it ever happened. Now go to bed, Jean. Bad as you feel now, you're going to feel worse in the morning."

And I had. I'd awakened sick and mortified, unable to recall a single thing that had happened after losing the basketball game to West High. I knew I'd done something unspeakable with a girl named Ellie, that I'd drunk alcohol and gotten in trouble, but the details seemed a blur and, when I tried to bring them into focus, my head hurt so bad that I felt nauseous all over again. But I remembered clearly my mother's warning, and like the good girl I'd been raised to be, I never mentioned Ellie's name again, neatly boxing the whole episode into a long-forgotten corner of my mind.

The bathwater was cold, my beer long gone, and still I sat in the tub, blinking back tears, pondering a truth so bold and glaring that I could no longer suppress it.

How could I have managed to block out something that significant? How had I managed to blame the whole shadowy memory on alcohol? Why had I allowed myself to forget the most memorable experience of my life?

I stood up and toweled off, rubbing at my goose bumps angrily, shaking my head at my blindness. It wasn't my mother I was so angry with all this time. It wasn't her ability to compartmentalize that infuriated me. It was my own. And with a sudden clarity that made me stand up taller than I'd stood for years, I not only understood who and what I was, but what I wanted to do with the rest of my life.

The Glen Abby Mortuary was packed. A media van had pulled up to the edge of the lawn and was filming the milling crowd as they made their way up the grassy slope to the graveside service. I hung back, nervous and excited at the same time. I hadn't told my parents I was coming. If I wanted to, I could turn around and drive back to Oregon right now. But I didn't want to. My stomach was in knots and my heart hammered erratically because moments earlier I'd heard someone whisper that the daughter, the one who'd been sent to the nut house as a teenager, was there.

I stood at the back of the crowd and half listened as the pastor murmured soothing words about the tragic loss of the loving couple. From where I stood I couldn't hear all of his words, but I could see Ellie Lane. Her head was bent, her short glossy black hair framing the smooth curve of neck that I remembered felt as smooth as satin.

Mesmerized and lost in memory, I nearly missed the announcement. The service had ended, and in a somber voice the pastor had invited friends of the family back to the house for a reception. As people turned and began to file past me, I stood, paralyzed. Then, before Ellie could spot me, I turned and blended in with the crowd.

I followed behind the procession of cars, not remembering where she'd lived exactly, but remembering well that it was on the west side of town where the rich people lived. I drove past the house and recognized it immediately, then found a spot half a block away, pulled up to the curb and turned off the engine. My hands were slick on the steering wheel and my throat felt dry. What if she didn't recognize me? What if she didn't want to see me? Worse, what if she didn't remember?

At this, I choked back a painful laugh. It was I who hadn't let myself remember her. But she'd been locked away for God knew how long. What if she wasn't the same? What if she'd found someone else?

I tortured myself for more than an hour, sitting in the sun-baked car. The longer I sat, the angrier I grew with myself. My mother was absolutely right — I *had* wasted my college years. I had been living a lie from the moment I agreed to forget about Ellie, and in the process I'd lost touch with myself.

Slowly, the anger I felt at myself turned to fear. I couldn't just traipse into her house after all this time and expect her to welcome me with open arms. Maybe I should wait a few days, until I could build up the courage to call her. On the other hand, maybe I should just turn around and drive back to Oregon before I made a complete fool of myself.

I turned the key in the ignition and threw the gear into reverse. Suddenly a shadow crossed the side window and I slammed on the brake, glancing up, startled. Ellie Lane leaned over and tapped on the glass. Heart thudding, I rolled down the window.

"Can't blame you for not wanting to come in. The place gives me the creeps too."

"Ellie." It was all I could manage.

"Bean." She reached in and brushed my cheek with the back of her hand.

"I — I'm sorry about what happened," I stammered. Her dark, maple eyes probed mine, finding the deeper meaning of my words. She was more beautiful than ever, I thought. The black blazer she wore suited her, matching the fine lashes and brow, the dark shiny hair. If anything, in the years since I'd seen her, she'd grown even more striking. Her eyes though, were the same deep pools that I remembered.

"Yeah, well. Me too." Her smile was so sad it touched me to the core. "You wouldn't by chance want to go somewhere, grab a Coke?"

"If I recall correctly, the last time you offered me a Coke, there was rum involved." The lightness of my voice masked the trembling I felt inside.

Ellie looked out at the gathering dusk, then glanced back, her eyes brimming with emotion. "Happen to know where we can pick some up," she said. "But I sure wish we had somewhere else to drink it. If I spend another minute in this town I'll start screaming and someone will think I've gone crazy." We both laughed at the irony.

"You like big, musty houses and lazy Abyssinians, by any chance?"

Ellie smiled, walked around to the passenger door

and slid in beside me. "What's an Abyssinian?" she asked, reaching over to lightly touch my leg. I shifted the car into gear and made a U-turn, heading out of town.

"Kind of like Motown, they grow on you. You'll see." I reached down and slid a cassette into the tape deck. Gladys Knight and the Pips filled the interior of the car, and Ellie started to laugh.

"It worked!" she shouted out the window. "I converted her!"

"In more ways than one," I said, knowing she couldn't hear me with her head thrust into the wind. It didn't matter, though. There'd be lots of time to explain. It was going to be a long, glorious ride home. I veered to the right and pulled over onto the shoulder, not caring who might drive by and see us. Ellie looked at me questioningly, but her surprise soon turned to a smile.

"Oh," she said.

"Exactly," I said. Then, knowing there weren't enough words in any language to make up for all that had happened, I pulled her to me and let my lips begin to explain the way I felt.

Remember Me

Ann O'Leary

It was close to seven p.m. on Friday when Holly
went into her dressing room and took a suit from
the wardrobe. It was black lightweight wool; the
perfectly tailored pants were fitted, and the long
fitted jacket had a Chinese collar. Gliding over her
skin, the deep pink pure silk lining felt cool and soft
as she put on the suit, buttoning the jacket. She put
on her gold watch. The taxi would arrive in thirty
minutes to take her to the annual Australian
Advertising Awards dinner. She slipped into black

patent leather high heels and went over to the mirrored dressing table.

Glancing at her nails, she checked that the deep-pink polish was immaculate, then applied a matching lipstick. With a sigh, she distractedly tugged at a few locks of her short blonde hair. She wasn't looking forward to the dinner. She had attended the Triple A function each year for the past fifteen years, usually picking up a couple of the prestigious awards, but the event no longer excited her. These days, as creative director of a large multinational agency, it was just something she was expected to do. Although she'd made some good friends over the years, she had found that advertising people en masse, once the alcohol and drugs kicked in, tended to behave like a pack of delinquents. It should really be the Alcoholics and Addicts Awards, she thought. Melting ice cubes crackled in the empty glass on her dressing table. There was probably time for another quick Campari. She picked up the glass and headed into the living room.

After fixing her drink at the solid walnut bar at one end of the spacious room, she wandered over to the window. Taking a cigarette from a pack on the lamp table beside the jade linen-covered sofa, she lit it, gazing outside. It was raining lightly. Her apartment was on the fifteenth floor of a steel-and-glass tower in Melbourne. The window was a full wall of tinted plate glass; there was no balcony, just a sheer drop that gave some visitors vertigo, but Holly liked standing there, right on the edge. The green expanse of the Royal Botanic Gardens spread out below her. Alongside it, an arterial road was clogged with cars pouring out of the city. On the horizon, between gathering swollen cobalt clouds, the remnants of a rust-colored sunset glimmered. It was the same rusty red of the northwest desert where Maxine lived, and remembering her, Holly's eyes filled with tears. She had met Max only three weeks ago in unlikely circumstances, in the unlikely setting of the Kimberley wilderness. The tranquillity of that place and the inspiration of Max's vision had begun to soak into the desert of Holly's mind, changing her forever. Tomorrow Max was leaving for Paris on her next adventure.

"Stay with me, come away with me," Max had breathed while Holly lay trembling in her arms. But Holly had lacked the courage to take the risks, to embrace the happiness that Max was offering.

She had done what she always did when career obligations collided with her personal life. She put work first. For fifteen years, since the age of twenty, she had focused her energy and dreams on success. As a junior copywriter she had believed that she only had to work hard, keep her ambition burning, and she would achieve everything she wanted. "Here you go, Holly," she had imagined some ponytailed executive would say one day, handing her a glittering, golden envelope. "Success! You've made it! Position, power, buckets of money, gorgeous cars and a happy life!"

She had it all except the happiness. Relationships had always been fleeting because she had never made time to nurture them. Before she met Max, she hadn't recognized that the emptiness in her life had begun to consume her. Since leaving her, the emptiness had become a constant dull ache. She pictured Max standing on the front porch of her desert cottage, her eyes wet with tears as Holly kissed her good-bye. "Remember me," Max had called out as Holly drove away.

Suddenly, the rain began to beat hard against the window; the scene became indistinct, the colors merging. The city was running in rivulets down the glass. Her boss, Simon, would be pumped up, eagerly awaiting the accolades tonight, she thought. As usual, in his falsely self-deprecating manner, he would manage to give the impression that he was personally responsible for the winning campaigns that Holly and her colleagues had slaved over. He was sneaky, lazy and dishonest in his dealing with clients, but he cleverly stroked the egos of the men who controlled the agency, and they liked him. For the past two years she had worked for him as creative director, having been lured back after quitting five years earlier. These days he pretty much kept out of her way, but it had been very different years ago when she was only a middle-weight writer and he was creative director. She remembered once, during one of their many disagreements, she had snapped at him, "You're depriving some poor village of an idiot! Do you know that!"

He had just grinned — like an idiot — and replied, "But I know who to hire to make me look good, sweetheart, and whose arses to kiss."

Holly drew on her cigarette, remembering how he used to hit on her too, and most of the other women in the office. It was irritating, but regarding Simon as a joke, they had all dismissed his ugly clumsy advances with a laugh. Everyone knew he'd never been in a relationship and that his sex education had been gleaned from the women he paid for and the collection of porn videos on a shelf in his office. He seemed quite unable to distinguish between fantasy and reality. But one night when Simon came into Holly's office and began breathing hotly on her shoulder, trailing his hand over her arse, Holly's patience had evaporated. "You know I'm a bloody dyke!" she yelled. "Why do you waste your time and annoy the hell out of me?"

Simon wasn't bothered. With a smarmy smile and the worldly confidence of a man who was sure of his facts, he said, "Oh, come on. I know you lesbians love screwing men."

She gazed at him in astonishment for a moment, then remembered noticing the video cover of *Lesbian Sluts' Gangbang* lying on top of the TV monitor in his office the day before. The cover photo featured two naked grinning blonde women surrounded by a dozen grinning men, dicks in hand. Holly rolled her eyes and sighed loudly. "Not the homosexual variety, you fuckwit!" she hissed. Finally fed up with his slimy advances and his incompetence, she had quit her job and walked out.

She had found another job within days. In the professional environment of the new agency with a talented supportive boss, challenging work and enthusiastic colleagues, Holly thrived. Not minding the ridiculous hours she worked, she was soon promoted to senior writer, won dozens of awards and her reputation soared. Meantime, her previous agency had been bought out by a multinational and, to Holly's disgust, Simon had been made managing director.

Two years ago he approached her with another job offer. Although by then the agency held accounts that made Holly's mouth water, she reminded herself that Simon was a bastard, that she was satisfied where she was and had a bright future. Before he had a chance to detail his offer, she said coolly, "Forget it! You're a dishonest, creepy little shit. *Nothing* would entice me to work for you again!"

Simon laughed. He shook with laughter. Wiping tears from his eyes, he said, "Oh yes it would, sweetheart. I want you as creative director."

Holly felt faint. There he was, the ponytailed executive handing her the golden envelope. Creative director! And she was only thirty! Prestige! Power! And a salary package that made her head spin. In her mind she slithered onto the floor, onto her back, and watched her soul slip out of her body to land in his outstretched, waiting hands as, breathlessly, she accepted his offer.

"That's the way, Holly," Simon had said smugly, glowing in triumph. "Didn't hurt, did it, sweetheart?"

Holly sipped her drink. It was growing dark quickly. Lights from cars, traffic signals and city buildings merged in glittery trails across the wet window. It had been a wet night like this when, one month ago, she had stood gazing out of the window, suddenly feeling breathless with a choking anxiety. The stress of her job had been building to the breaking point, and the urge to escape it for a while was overwhelming. Wanting to get as far away as possible, the remoteness of the Kimberley region of northwest Australia appealed, and two days later she took off for a week's break.

The beautiful pearling town of Broome was perched on the brim of the Indian Ocean, edged by miles of soft white sand to the east, and bordered by red desert to the west. It provided peaceful relief for a few days. Holly basked in the hot sun and relaxed in the cooling sea breezes. But it wasn't long before she began to feel restless. Without any clear purpose but impatient to be doing something, she hired a car and drove out of Broome's tropical gardens, into the desert. Heading south, she had a vague idea of stopping at coastal towns along the way. Gradually, the grassy plains gave way to desolate red earth. Stands of boab trees, their stout bottle-shaped trunks bloated with stored water, shimmered in the heat haze. The next town was farther than she thought; the road seemed to stretch ahead forever. After an hour the isolation began to feel oppressive.

Suddenly, the horizon began to move. Distant hills etched in stark peaks against the blue sky became misty and obscure. In sheets, the sand peeled off the plains around her, whipped up by a powerful roaring wind. Within minutes Holly was unable to see, and she pulled off the road. With the windows wound up, the wind howling and the red desert airborne, blotting out the sky, she waited anxiously.

Then, as suddenly as it began the windstorm ceased. Hovering sand dropped back onto the plains, the sky reappeared — stained red, streaked with gold. The car was like an oven. She got out and wandered a short distance. A few tufts of coarse pale grass stubbornly gripped the earth; a lizard slunk under a rock. Breathlessly, Holly looked around her. She couldn't get a grip on the place. Her mind whirled with tidy compact images of boardrooms, restaurants, apartments, streets that led to other streets, taxis, crowds.

While she stood feeling dwarfed and alien in that wilderness, she wondered whether to go back to Broome or push ahead. Then she heard a car approaching. In a dust cloud, a utility vehicle pulled off the road. The driver got out and crossed the road toward her. Through the swirling dust, Holly glimpsed broad tanned shoulders, a khaki tank top, and faded jeans slung low on slim hips. A black peaked cap hid the stranger's face.

The dust settled, revealing the stranger to be a woman. She stood by Holly's car, dropped a dazzling smile and pulled off her dark wrap sunglasses. "You'll fry, standing out here," she said in a husky voice. Shifting her weight onto one leg, she leaned a hip against Holly's car. Her eyes were sky blue; the wisps of hair that showed beneath her cap were dark. "Car trouble?" she asked, casually brushing some sand from the windscreen of Holly's car.

Holly walked over to her. "No. I just stopped for the dust storm. I should keep going before it gets dark."

"You won't make it to the next town before that. Here, when night falls, it's black as pitch in minutes."

Holly hesitated. The desolation was lonely enough in daylight; she didn't want to be driving after dark.

"Do you have to meet someone?" the woman

asked. Holly shook her head, suddenly painfully conscious that she had no one to meet and no purpose at all in hurtling headlong down the highway. The woman looked at her searchingly, then smiled again. "My name's Maxine. Max. My place is twenty minutes from here. Back toward Broome." She gestured eastward. "Inland a bit . . . on a cattle station. It's probably safer for you to continue in the morning if you're not in a rush. I'd like the company if you'd be my guest for the night."

Holly was taken aback. Maxine chuckled. "Don't be shocked. Out here, people watch out for one another. And jump at the chance to have some good company." With a touch of shyness, she twisted her small gold earring. "It's been a long time since I shared dinner with a beautiful woman."

Max was attractive, her warm expression intelligent and enticing, and Holly admired her nerve. Why not? she thought. She would enjoy the distraction of some company herself. She smiled. "Thanks. I'd like that."

She followed Max's Ford Utility back up the highway a short distance, then along a private road that took her through scrubby bushland and across dry creek beds. Soon the bush gave way to more open, rolling red plains and gently undulating hills. Suddenly, a green oasis came into view; a faded red iron roof peeped through a tangle of treetops, and a tall windmill spun slowly. Max's truck turned off the road onto a dirt track that led into the driveway of the cottage.

Holly got out of her car and looked around in amazement. The driveway was covered with a cool canopy of trees. A brick path led through a tangle of red hibiscus, tall banksia trees laden with golden cones, and in the dank shady places, hydrangeas and camellias bloomed in pink and white. The house was simple, like a box with a veranda tacked on the front. It leaned slightly to the left but shone with fresh white paint. Carrying a box of groceries, Max led her into the house. The kitchen was dominated by a large scrubbed wooden table. Against one wall, an old pine cupboard with wire-mesh doors served as a pantry. Protected from the sun, the house was surprisingly cool. A large window revealed a luxuriant back garden replete with vegetable beds. Above the greenery, the red desert hills loomed. Max offered her a fresh lime juice, pouring two glasses from a frosty jug she took from the small fridge. "From my own lime trees," she said. "Come on outside. I'll show you my tower."

Built onto the back of the house was a simple wooden scaffold, painted dark green, with a platform at roof level surrounded by two rails. They climbed up the fixed ladder at one side and sat down on wicker chairs. For a second, Holly's stomach somersaulted nervously as she surveyed the view. In every direction, there was nothing but a few stands of boabs and clumps of gray eucalypti here and there. How could anyone bear this emptiness? she wondered. Max was gazing into the distance with a relaxed smile. A warm breeze blew in off the desert, and the trees murmured. Maxine pulled off her cap, and an unexpected mass of long, shining, dark brown hair fell around her muscled shoulders. She was breathtaking.

"Look at that sunset," Max said softly.

Holly tore her gaze away from Max and stared at
the sky, washed orange, marbled with gold. Anxious
to relate, to find some perspective in that vastness,
Holly narrowed her eyes, taking in the view like a
camera. A mid-shot of a pair of Bollé sunglasses came
to mind. Lying as if casually tossed on a sandy hill,
they would reflect that astonishing sky in their dark
lenses, the Bollé logo, bottom right, could fade up
slowly as if emerging from the sand, a wind machine
could blow a controlled wisp of red earth over the
glasses, an eerie wind sound effect could run behind
the intimate voice-over. A nice little TV spot, Holly
thought, feeling calmer.

She became aware that Max was watching her,
smiling. "Bit jumpy, aren't you," Max said. Holly
realized that she was tapping her fingernails on the
side of her glass. She shrugged self-consciously. "I
used to be like that," Max added. She stood and
stretched. Tall, her athletic body rippled, her skin
glowed bronze like the hills. She shook her hair back
like a pony tossing its mane, and it shimmered titian
for a moment. "Let's cook dinner. I'm starving."

In the kitchen, Max opened a bottle of ice-cold
Chablis and poured it into long-stemmed crystal
glasses. She had bought some fresh ocean trout in a
town on the coast and, while Holly sat comfortably at
the table watching her, Max, with unhurried ease,
prepared a stuffing of finely chopped bacon, pine
nuts, breadcrumbs and shallots. The wind rustled the
leaves outside the window, and birds feeding in the
fruit trees chattered while Holly sipped her wine.

"You're obviously not originally from these parts,"
Holly said. Max's accent was eastern like hers. "Why

do you live alone all the way out here?" Max placed the ingredients in a cast-iron pan on the stove, and the smell of the sizzling bacon and pine nuts made Holly suddenly feel hungry.

"I wanted to change my life. I just wandered up this way from Melbourne about eighteen months ago without any clear plans, looking for a new challenge really. I was a computer programmer for a bank." Max removed the pan from the stove, spooned the stuffing into the fish, wrapped them in foil and placed them in the oven. "I just followed the road off the highway and found this cottage, abandoned and badly run-down. It was a stockman's house years ago before the big drought came. A wealthy family owns the station — hundreds of miles of land. Their cattle are in another more fertile part of the Kimberley. I contacted the owners, and they said I was welcome to live here, and they were glad of my offer to fix it up."

Holly was bewildered. She asked Max how she could stand the hardship, how she knew what to do.

Max sat down at the table and, looking at Holly, drank some wine. There was a depth in her gaze that Holly hadn't seen in anyone for years. "For ten years I designed banking programs. Whenever they thought up some new product, I was one of the people who figured out how to implement it. I really liked it for a while, but although each project was different in detail, I'd mastered the principles of the work. I could do it . . . you know? I got bored. I started to worry that all I knew was that job. I didn't know how to do anything else, and my forays out into the wider world were limited to a few

weeks' vacation each year. I worked long hours; I was
obsessive and competitive. I was unhappy and could
never settle into a serious relationship." She
shrugged. "It wasn't a future I could look forward
to." She got up to mix a salad. Max's words were
unsettling. They articulated a notion that felt familiar
but hadn't yet taken form in Holly's mind. "It was
dreadful at first. The only thing I had was water
from the underground bore — the windmill worked
okay. I got some bottled gas to run the stove and
fridge, then some solar panels for hot water and
power. I bought books and learned how to do things."
Max grinned happily. "I loved it all. Figuring out how
to solve problems, having only my own resources to
call on. I learned how to cook, and, so that I could
enjoy the panoramic views, I even built my tower!"

The amber light suddenly dropped, and Max
switched on a lamp. Then she served dinner on
beautiful white Wedgewood plates. Her loose khaki
top slipped off one glossy brown shoulder, and Holly
was conscious of her earthy sexuality. She smiled at
Max, thinking how delightfully decadent it felt to be
drinking excellent wine from those beautiful glasses
and eating from plates of translucent fine china at a
rough old table in that simple homey cottage with a
lean.

In the middle of the desert, no less.

As if reading her thoughts, Max held up her glass,
watching it glint in the lamplight. "I've found that
many of the possessions I used to think were essen-
tial aren't important at all," she said, smiling, "but
I'm very fussy about the things I have close to my
body." For the first time in more than a year — since

her last girlfriend, Jodie, had walked out, Holly felt a delicious erotic warmth stir in her body as she held Max's gaze.

Max asked Holly about her life. While Holly told her about her job — there wasn't much else to tell — Max listened with apparent interest, her gaze moving slowly over Holly's face, lingering sometimes on her mouth, making Holly's heart race.

"You enjoy your work, then?"

Holly hesitated. Enjoy? The question came as a shock. She realized that it had been a long time since she'd taken any real pleasure in her work. She had, after all, been doing the same thing for years. "Keeps me busy," she had murmured.

Dragging her thoughts back to the present, Holly glanced at her watch. Seven-thirty. She gulped down the rest of her drink. It was time to leave for the award dinner.

The reception area outside the function room at the Regent Hotel in the heart of Melbourne was packed. Laughter pealed above the din of attention-seeking anecdotes and bitchy one-liners. Brilliant white smiles flashed like glinting daggers. Enormous chandeliers shimmered overhead. Eyes flickered everywhere at once, catching who was there, who wasn't, who was somebody, who was nobody, who was sucking up, who was backstabbing, and who was screwing whom, and all the while white-suited, tray-bearing waiters flitted in and out of the shoal of dinner suits and black dresses like fish through a net.

Taking a glass of Champagne from a passing tray, Holly took a large gulp. Looking around, she dropped mandatory smiles in response to teeth bared in her direction. Oh, God. Simon had spotted her and was coming over.

"Holly!" Loud, beaming and overexcited, he almost forgot himself and nearly kissed her cheek. But above her fixed smile he caught her icy glare and stopped himself in time. Sniffing, he gave his nose a quick rub. He'd probably just done a line of coke, Holly thought, relieved. He was slightly less irritating when he did drugs. "We're going to clean up tonight, sweetheart!" he said. "We'll pick up some new business out of this for sure!" As usual, his voice boomed, and heads turned to look, which was just what he wanted. Holly glanced at the bored-looking woman beside him. "Oh, you must meet . . . umm . . . Delilah." He faltered over her name, apparently having some trouble remembering it. Delilah didn't seem to care. Like all the one-off dates Simon had appeared with over the years, she had the distracted detached air of a bought one.

Holly extended her hand. "Delighted, Delilah," she said, snatching a glance at Simon. He cleared his throat, stuffed his hands into his pockets and feigned interest in something fascinating supposedly happening over Holly's shoulder. Delilah's long red silicone nails brushed Holly's palm, her blue cellophane gaze sweeping over Holly's Chanel suit as her mouth twitched in some semblance of a smile. With a barely audible sigh, she stole a peek at the clock on the wall. It's not over yet, Delilah, Holly thought. Like herself, Delilah clearly wished she was elsewhere.

"See you in the dining room later," Simon said, obviously keen to leave Holly's derisive glares and find someone who didn't know what a fraud he was. Clutching Delilah's hand like a shopping bag, his plastic grin homing in on some poor hapless person, Simon slithered away to mingle.

Holly gulped at the Champagne growing warm in her hand — the bubbles forcing down the anxiety rising to her throat as she stared at the crowd around her. She had felt the same unease when she first found herself in the desert. She could feel herself merging with its emptiness and begin to disappear. Unlike Max who seemed to fill it. Holly imagined that even the sandy earth stirred under her gaze, the trees quivered at the warmth of her laughter, and the birds stopped to listen when she spoke. In charge of her own destiny, Max couldn't be bought because what she craved wasn't included in any golden envelopes proffered by ponytailed executives. Her ambition was happiness, and she had achieved it. Max, in her leaning cottage in the middle of nowhere, had succeeded where Holly, chasing the wrong dream, had failed.

"Holly, darling!" Timothy was waving his hand above the crowd, bravely hacking his way through the Versace jungle as he headed over to her. She smiled, glad to see him. They had teamed together at Holly's previous agency and become friends. A talented art director, Holly had brought him with her when she took up her new job, making him sub-creative director. They worked together on the bigger campaigns. "The flowers are *gorgeous!*" he gushed, hugging her. Knowing how nervous he was about the awards, she had sent him a box of cut flowers that afternoon. "Fucking *huge* box full!" he said, gesturing wildly. "Big as a baby's coffin, darling!" Holly chuckled as he kissed her cheek.

Dinner was being served, and they made their way into the grand dining room where waiters ushered them to their tables. Some other members of Holly's creative staff joined them, and while they chatted excitedly among themselves, as Simon sniffled and guffawed — his eyes glassy — and Delilah suppressed yawns, Holly's mind drifted back to the desert.

"I've achieved what I came here to do. Got my act together," Max had said over dinner. "I'm ready for something new. I'm leaving in a few weeks." She smiled, her eyes glittering in the lamplight. "I'm going to Paris, taking the Orient Express to Rome, then going on to Tuscany. There's a little villa I'm heading for in San Vincenzo on the coast. I plan on being in the town square, drinking local wine, watching fireworks when the new millennium arrives." Holly's heart sank. The thought that she may never see Max again came as a shock. Incredulous, she asked Max how she was going to make a living in the longer term. Max chuckled, gave a carefree shrug and replied, "Who knows? I sold my house and invested the money, so that should keep me out of trouble for a while. But I know now that I can almost do anything I put my mind to. I want to try things that interest me. I know I'll be okay."

The idea of simply abandoning the conventions of an accepted stable lifestyle would normally have seemed irresponsible to Holly, but there was nothing irresponsible about Max. She was beginning to sound like the most stable person Holly had ever met. She was certainly the most desirable. As the evening progressed, Max's penetrating gaze became increasingly intimate and sexual. The heat inside Holly grew, spreading through her body like a slow fire until her skin burned. She accepted Max's invitation to stay for the remaining few days of her vacation, and when Max said good-night, kissing her cheek, Holly trembled.

The second evening after dinner, they sat in Max's tower under a star-filled sky drinking coffee and Cognac. "And what are your plans for the future?" Max asked. Holly hesitated. More of the same, she thought, her heart sinking. "What are you looking forward to?" Max prompted.

Holly shrugged. "Eventually I'll probably be made an associate director." She wondered about the possibility of ever taking over Simon's job, and had to admit that no matter how hard she worked, the chances were slim. And she wondered for the first time whether she would want that job anyway. Apart from more money, which she didn't need, she couldn't imagine any real gains. Her creative talents would become irrelevant; she would spend her days and most evenings negotiating business deals and entertaining clients, which was of little interest to her, constantly juggling favors and watching her back. It certainly wouldn't fulfill her yearning for happiness.

"Great! If that's what you want." Max was watching her. Her white T-shirt glowed in the light of the kerosene lamp, her cutoff jeans displaying her gorgeous long legs stretched out in front of her.

"No, I don't want that!" Holly suddenly blurted, surprising herself. Tears sprang to her eyes. "I want time for things. Time to think." The words tumbled out like a confession. "I want to know what it's like to go to a concert and become absorbed, read a book and be enthralled, make love and be transported!" Unstoppable, the tears trickled down her cheeks. "I want to be involved, deep inside things, not going through the motions. I want to get my mind off the ground." She stared at the moon-washed desert, and its vastness, no longer formidable, seemed to beckon her. Then Max's arms were around her, drawing her to her feet. Max's breathing was shallow; there was a quivering tension in her muscles, and when Holly looked into her eyes, they were dark and passionate. A powerful desire erupted within Holly, sweeping through her like a storm, and they kissed.

On white cotton sheets that smelled of the sun, Holly lay naked, gasping as Max kissed her throat, then trailed her tongue down to her breasts. Holly groaned, urgently wanting more. She reached for Max but she caught Holly's hands, kissing them. "There's no hurry," she whispered. Gently holding Holly's wrists down against the bed, Max slowly alternated her kisses between Holly's mouth and her breasts. Whimpering, Holly was desperate for sweet release. But Max, her heart pounding against Holly's body, was taking her time; she seemed to be waiting for something. Just when Holly thought she couldn't stand the agonizing tension any longer, she felt herself swept up to another plane. Her body stilled, her mind calmed and she floated, charged with an exquisite sensuality. As if from the depths of a dream, merging with the distant cries of the wind across the desert, she heard Maxine murmur, "Now . . ." Her hair trailed over Holly's stomach. "Oh, God . . ." Max breathed as her mouth took Holly; her tongue moving slowly in melting strokes until Holly felt her body dissolve.

Bouncing off the hills, the tangerine dawn light seeped through the bedroom window, and Maxine whispered, "Come with me to Paris. We can explore our lives together, go anywhere, do anything. I love you." Holly's mind shimmered with the exciting possibilities of wandering together wherever their whim took them, becoming absorbed in the rhythms of other worlds. It contrasted with images of her past hurried travels. She had watched donkeys carrying goats in saddlebags up the hills in Hydra, stood on the wrought-iron balcony of a tiny hotel in Venice watching the fog lift over the Grand Canal, sipped coffee in Paris watching people promenade up and down the Champs Élysées. But she had always been only watching, standing on the edge.

Then Simon called her mobile phone to tell her that problems had arisen at work. She had to return to Melbourne right away. Suddenly, like the veil of a dream had been snatched away, her love for Max and all their idyllic talk seemed unrealistic, impossible. Fifteen years of single-minded dedication had her jumping back into work mode like a trained monkey, and she had left.

Timothy grabbed her. "It's us, darling!" he shrieked. Holly blinked in the spotlight that was holding them both captive. Applause crashed in her head. Timothy was standing, dragging at her hand, the presenter was on the stage beaming at her, the wall of video screens flickered with their Vogue Australia TV campaign, and the music they'd spent weeks recording and endlessly remixing pulsed behind the applause. "Advertising Award of the year, Holly!" Timothy said breathlessly. "The *big* one, darling! We've won fucking *gold!*"

Disoriented, Holly walked with him up the steps onto the stage. Gazing at the crowd — a blur beyond the stage lights — Holly's eyes filled with tears. Coming back here was a huge mistake. She wanted Maxine. Her heart aching, she murmured a few appropriate words as the golden award was handed to her. They stood in quiet reverence as the campaign was played again.

From the corner of her eye, Holly saw someone move in front of the stage then sit in a chair in the glow of the footlights. She turned to look and nearly fainted. Dressed in a beautiful black dinner suit, her hair tumbling over her shoulders, Max grinned up at her. Holly's heart leapt. She could hardly believe her eyes! Holding Holly's gaze, Max took something from her breast pocket and held it up for Holly to see. An airline ticket — Air France. With a flick of her fingers, a second ticket fanned out behind the first. Through her tears, Holly saw Max chuckle then mouth the words, "Remember me?"

Bursting with happiness, Holly turned to Timothy. "Do you want my job?" she whispered. He looked

bewildered. "Would it make you happy?" Dazed, he
nodded. "It's yours." She pressed the award into his
hands and gave him a hug. "Good-bye Timothy, and
good luck." The campaign was still playing as she
began to walk off the stage. Max was standing at the
foot of the steps, waiting for her.

"Where are you going?" Timothy hissed anxiously.

Holly chuckled. "Paris."

"When are you coming back?"

Holly gave a carefree shrug. "Who knows?" Max
reached up to her and Holly took her hand. She gave
Timothy a parting smile. "Remember me."

Who Will Cry for
the Snake?
Catherine Ennis

How many times do I have to tell you? She'll be dead before morning, and that's all I know!" Howard's voice, usually a persistent whine, was now authori- tative. He was in charge. He was the one the doctors came to when something needed to be signed, when personal decisions were required. "So, are you coming or not? And if so, when?"

Peg swiveled her chair and stared, unseeing, out the window, stunned at the suddenness of this announcement with no preliminary warnings.

"I can't wait all day, Peg. I have a death-watch to keep! If she regains consciousness again, shall I tell her you're on your way?"

Peg stifled a tiny giggle at the thought of a dying Harriet gathering her bedclothes about her and running screaming from the room at the thought of such an unwanted visit from her stepdaughter at such an inconvenient moment.

"I'll be there as soon as I can, Howard. I'll come straight to the hospital before checking in to the Norton Inn."

Always before, when they needed something from her, Howard and his mother had stood together, wearing her down, building themselves up by be-littling her. Now, he would have to face her alone when he needed more money, and somehow make it sound like it was something she owed him.

She stared though the glass at the soft shadows that moved with the afternoon sun. She pictured the thin face of the old woman . . . thin lips curled downward, eyes hooded and full of hate.

Turning back to the desk, she reached for the phone and touched the numbers almost without looking. The ringing was loud and clear. "Please be there," she whispered into the mouthpiece. "Please be home."

After five or six rings, there was a click, then a breathless voice. "Hello!"

"Linda?" As if it could be anyone else.

"Peg! What's wrong, darling? You sound strange."

"Howard called. My stepmother's dying. I have to go."

There was a brief pause. "Dying of what? This is awfully sudden!"

"Cancer. She's not expected to last the night."

"Peg, people don't just up and die of cancer. It usually takes a long time. Did Howard say how long she's known?"

Peg closed her eyes and sighed. She heard again her stepbrother's voice running on and on about surgery and chemotherapy, and losing hair, and about having hope and then no hope.

"About a year, I think."

"Why did they never mention it until now?"

"I guess they didn't need anything from me."

"So I'll bet Howard's beginning to feel insecure about the house he has always lived in rent-free, tax-free, repair-free ...."

"Please, Linda, let's not rehash all that. I'm leaving the shop now. I'm coming home just long enough to pack for a couple of days and a funeral."

"Okay, I'll start preparations. You hurry home to me now."

Judy came into the office in answer to Peg's summons.

"What's wrong, Peg?"

Without turning, Peg answered, "My stepmother's dying and I have to go. Will you take care of things here? You know as much about the business as I do."

"Sure, hon, you know I will. Is there anything else I can do?"

If there are any questions and you can't reach me, call Linda. She'll locate me if necessary."

"You can count on me, on all of us, you know that. Don't give this place a second thought."

They walked together downstairs and into the huge bookstore. An archway led into a smaller room crowded with art supplies. Both rooms were busy; customers looking through counters and shelves of books, waiting at registers, selecting paints and posters, and clerks moving purposefully.

"A good day, as usual." Judy sounded pleased.

Peg smiled absently, already dreading Linda's comments and the long drive.

Peg drove carefully, moving through city traffic to the expressway, traveling slightly over the posted speed. A kaleidoscope of images filled her mind. Trusting herself to make the correct moves, she drove with the stream of traffic that was beginning to swell with afternoon rush.

Automatically taking the correct exit, she guided the car through a series of turns to a narrow paved road, tree lined with oak limbs touching overhead.

She slowed and turned again onto a shady but narrower unpaved lane that wound through huge azaleas in full bloom. Today, however, she was too preoccupied to appreciate the beauty their loving work and nurturing had wrought.

Peg stopped the car with a crunch of gravel, slowly opened the door and got out before turning to look at the house and the figure waiting on the brick-floored veranda.

There was always a special thrill of anticipation when she first saw Linda again, no matter how brief the separation had been, but today it was mixed with the slight dread of having to listen to what Linda thought of Howard and Harriet . . . and indeed anyone who did not properly appreciate her darling Peg.

She walked across the drive into Linda's waiting arms.

"Oh, honey, I didn't mean to fuss at you. You know that, don't you?" Linda was contrite. "It's only that they always manage to hurt you ... I don't want you to be hurt!"

Peg touched her lips to the shining auburn hair. "I know, darling, but please just let me pick up a few things and be on my way ... no lectures, please."

"Where will you stay while you're in town? I don't suppose they even offered to allow you to stay in your own house?"

"No, it wasn't mentioned. You know how Ethel feels about having me around the twins ... being a pervert and all ..." Peg shrugged.

Linda's mouth opened slightly, but seeing Peg's misery, she just took her hand and led her though the open door.

"I haven't had time to pack for you, but your suitcase is on your bed and I'm making sandwiches so you can eat along the way without an extra stop." Linda moved toward the kitchen, finishing the thought under her breath as she adjusted her apron. "It'll be a cold day in hell before any of them feed you. Most likely that bunch of freeloaders will want you to feed them ... all they want is everything you own ..." She gritted her teeth as she trimmed the bread. "I've got a good mind to go with you. I'd like to see them pick at you with me around!" This was clearly such a satisfying thought that Linda was grinning as she poured hot coffee into a thermos.

Not really caring, Peg went into the bedroom and began pulling assorted items of clothing from drawers and closets and dropping them into her small suit-case. Then, overcome with memories of her early teen years living in the house that had ceased to be a home after her father's death, living with that shrew, Harriet, and her weasel of a son.

She relived that awful day when she was fifteen and heard Harriet's hateful voice, "What are you doing, you filthy girl? You dirty little pervert! You get out of this house, you filth. You don't live here any-more with decent people!"

Peg remembered her own feeble voice, reedy with surprise, trying to insert words of protest into the stream of unexpected and uncalled for accusations. She did not understand how the innocent embrace of her best friend could, in any way, be related to this venomous attack.

Peg had found herself standing in stunned silence in front of her house. (It was her house. Her father had seen to that.) She still wore the sneakers and shorts she had worn to tennis practice earlier. Her shirtsleeves were wet from wiping tears, and she was clutching a canvas duffel bag zipped over a few stray items of clothing (collected with about the same thought as those in the suitcase on her bed now).

She had stood there trying to decide what to do, where to go, while Harriet stood on the front porch, her voice filling Peg's world, telling all those in it what a filthy, lowdown pervert she was. Howard watched gleefully from the front window as he, too, mouthed the words he heard his mother scream.

"Are you going over it again, honey?" Linda's voice interrupted the painful memories. She crossed to the bed and bent to touch Peg's lips with her own. "I know you want to do this by yourself, Peg, but let me go with you and stay in the motel. No one has to know I'm even there."

Seeing the concern on Linda's face, Peg embraced her gently but said decidedly, "No I'll go alone and do what convention demands, take care of business and hurry back home to you." She paused. "I don't know why I hate her so much. She couldn't take the house away and keep it. I didn't miss the money they've wanted from time to time, and I was so much happier living with Aunt Ruth."

"I just don't understand why you've let them walk all over you all these years and why you think you owe them anything." Linda bit her lip as if to keep from saying more.

"Maybe it's because I turned out to be exactly what she thought I was. To her thinking, it was a shameful thing and she was right to send me away." She sighed. "After I finished school and Aunt Ruth died, I moved around so much I never knew where I belonged . . . I was always afraid to get close to any-one . . . until I met you, that is."

Peg smiled, remembering the afternoon Linda had come into the store to order art supplies and stayed past closing, her dark hair almost falling on the page as together they poured over catalogs, their shoulders touching, enclosed in a warm circle of light.

"I didn't mean to get you started, Peg, but you're going to get there and they'll want money for the hospital and money for the funeral and money for house repairs and . . . It's your money and I know you have it to spare. It's not the money really, but what it represents. They walk all over you and take advantage of your good nature. Look, I want you to do what you think you have to do. What I don't want is for you to feel that you're at fault for Howard being so stupid or for her having cancer."

"I won't. I promise."

"All right, now let's see what you've packed in here . . ." Linda calmly folded and repacked what Peg had chosen, adding other things as she thought of them. Finally she closed the bag and turned to Peg.

"I don't really want to go," Peg said bleakly. "I just have to . . . this one last time."

"Come home as soon as you can and don't drive too fast, and remember I love you."

Peg watched Linda in the rearview mirror until the azalea blooms filled the glass. Then, in a spurt of speed, she turned onto the roadway and slowed only to enter the interstate.

Her mind was so filled with painful memories that she almost missed her exit. Now so near the little town, she began to think about the woman who was to die. Everyone in town would be at the funeral home. She knew from other funerals that the men would stand outside the building, smoking and talking. The women would be inside, sitting straight on little sofas, talking and crying. There would be a lot of crying. It was expected that the women would cry . . . no matter how much they may have disliked the deceased, having known her for most of their lives. Dying automatically made you worthy of being grieved loudly and enthusiastically.

Peg could see the stuffy little parlor, the open coffin, the wall of cut flowers with their stifling odor. She could hear the wailing. Howard would cry. Ethel would cry. The twin girls would cry. All those tears, and not a drop of genuine grief among them!

Peg touched the brakes to avoid getting too close to a slower vehicle that had swerved to the right ahead of her, almost running off the pavement. What caused them to do that? she wondered. Then she saw that the driver had swerved to hit a snake. The reptile lay writhing in the road.

Poor thing, Peg thought, dying on the roadside, alone, in pain . . . and no one knows or cares. She aimed her wheels at the creature and felt a slight hump as the car hit first with its front wheels and then with the back.

"At least it's dead now . . . no more pain."

She shuddered, thinking of all those people crying fake tears for Harriet who had been cruel and uncaring all her life. She thought of the snake, probably harmless, innocent of intent or desire except for the little warmth it could absorb from the pavement. She asked aloud, "Who'll cry for the snake?"

She slowed the car and pulled over to the side of the road. Finally the tears came . . . great wrenching sobs dammed up for so long came in torrents forming a flood that swept away the hurt and any implied sense of guilt . . . tears for her mother who had left the earth when Peg was an infant . . . tears for her father who left just as she was reaching puberty . . . tears for the injustice of the accusations and abandonment by her stepmother . . . tears for every injustice suffered by anyone . . . and tears for the snake who asked nothing and died just the same.

Finally, the flow dwindled and ended with a few sniffles and a new resolve. She was done with her grieving. Harriet would have to do without her fake tears and Howard wouldn't have her support every time he wanted something he wasn't willing to work for on his own.

She said aloud, "I'm going home to Linda now, and I'm leaving tears behind me."

She turned the car and headed back down the road.

There Comes a Time
Jackie Calhoun

I see clearly now what I was blind to then. The thought of her emerges from the smoke screen of denial that characterized my youth and taunts me. When she called the other day after twenty-eight years of silence to say she'd be in town, could we have lunch, I felt such a longing that I wanted as much to run from it as I did toward her.

Looking in the mirror at an older version of myself, I wonder how she has fared with age. I was so green, so young, so stupid then. It took me twenty-three years to admit to myself that marriage was not for me and another three to get out of it. By then my children were grown.

I fancy I like living alone. The one relationship I forged with another woman ended badly a few months ago. I promise myself I won't take that risk again easily.

Walking toward the Thai restaurant through a gloomy April day, the wet wind at my back, excitement and anxiety battled within for the upper hand. When I reached the door, I felt slightly sick.

The dark restaurant was alive with the babble of voices. The hostess asked if I want to be seated, and I looked beyond her into the dining room. From a booth on the other side, Clara stood and waved.

We sat across from each other, smiling a little shyly, and it all came back to me.

I met Clara during my junior year at a small Indiana university, when we roomed across the hall from each other at Manley Manor. She'd been kicked out of her sorority because of poor grades. I'd never pledged.

I cut classes regularly and, when I wasn't sleeping or eating or socializing, I spent my time absorbed in fiction. Every year from the age of sixteen, I reread *The Catcher in the Rye,* my favorite book. Holden Caulfield reminded me of my cousin, a rebel who made me laugh.

Clara, who came from a wealthy family, slept most of her days away. She awoke late afternoons, in time to go out with her boyfriend, Dean, whom I disliked. I saw him as snobbish, controlling, a real fraternity boy, someone I suspected was after the family money. Outside of myself, she was the most confused person I knew.

I hailed from a state with beer bars that catered to eighteen-year-olds, and I chafed against the strict rules of this small, Bible Belt, church-oriented school, where the girls were required to wear skirts on campus and be in residence by ten-thirty during the week and twelve-thirty on weekends. There were no hours for male students, and no dress code. All my life I'd found offensive the stiffer set of rules society imposed on the female sex.

One night after a fight with her boyfriend, Clara knocked on my dorm door. I was lying on my bed reading a paperback and listening to music. I sat up cross-legged as she came in. She had eyes like a doe and wavy brown hair. I don't think she knew what a beauty she was.

Her eyes and nose were red from crying. "What are you up to?" she asked.

Earlier I'd set aside the textbook on sociology I'd been studying, because it sent me into a coma. "Not much."

"Thought you had a test tomorrow."

"I do. I'll have to fake it. Maybe it'll be an essay." I always did well when given the chance to bullshit in a blue book. A little knowledge could be expanded in a lot of ways. But I knew the exam would probably be multiple choice or fill in the blanks or true and false, and I'd be lost.

She came over and sat on the bed. "Dean's always nagging at me about my grades. He wants me back in the sorority. I think I embarrass him."

Appearances were important to Dean. I sat up straighter and cleared my throat but said nothing. Even I knew she couldn't skip so many classes and spend so much time sleeping and make her grades.

She burst into tears. "They're going to kick me out at the end of the semester."

I realized they might be kicking me out too. Lighting up a cigarette and thinking of Holden, I said, "Want to beat them to the punch?" It was a couple of weeks before Christmas break, about the time Caulfield bolted from prep school.

"What?"

"Want to go to Naptown for a few days?"

"And do what?" she asked.

I shrugged. "Have some fun."

She grinned, showing beautiful white teeth. "When?"

"Tomorrow."

We took the bus. There is nothing drearier than a Greyhound station in the dead of winter, yet I felt a thrill of excitement. My fellow classmates would be sitting down to the sociology test right now. Breaking the rules like this gave me a taste of delicious freedom.

"Dean's going to kill me," Clara said with a giggle as we setttled into our seats halfway down the aisle. "And I don't care. For once, I'm wide awake."

"Me too," I said, looking out the window at the dingy little town we were leaving.

She slept most of the way there, however. When I tired of reading, I watched the flat farm fields flash by.

We hissed into the station in Indy and took a taxi to a hotel we looked up in a phone book. The Circle downtown blazed with Christmas decorations. Colored lights, strung from the tip of Miss Indiana to the ground below, shook in the wind. At the foot of the statue stood a large manger scene. In one department store window, a toy train chugged through a miniature town laid out on cotton batting. In another, animated elves worked around a mechanized Santa, loading his sleigh with toys.

A Christmas tree dominated the lobby of the hotel. By then, though, I was feeling guilty and a little scared. I envisioned myself all too soon boarding the Monon, the college train that rolled the length of the state of Indiana, and transferring to the Chicago and Northwestern in the Windy City for the final leg home where I would have to face my parents and somehow prepare them for my failing grades.

Lying on the double bed in the hotel, we smoked Viceroy cigarettes and talked, and I again experienced a joyful burst of freedom. For once, I was answerable to no one.

"Let's buy some beer tonight," I suggested.

"Yeah," she said. "Let's get drunk out of our minds."

We wandered the aisles of L.S. Ayres and Blocks, while carols heralded through the overhead speakers. Clara tried on clothes and purchased a couple of sweaters. I bought presents for my parents and sisters. Attendants at Salvation Army kettles rang bells and stamped their feet. Fastened high on lamp-posts, garlands of gold stars and angels shuddered as a damp wind swept through the streets, chasing us into sheltering doorways and stores.

Clara had managed somehow to stay in college long enough to reach her senior year. She had turned twenty-one in November. While I waited outside, she went into a package liquor store and bought two six-packs of cold Budweiser. At the hotel, we took the stairs to our third-floor room.

We had grabbed a late lunch at a greasy restaurant: french fries and hamburgers, which we'd washed down with Pepsis. Now I popped the lid on one of the beers and quaffed greedily. I flopped down on the bed with Clara and turned on the TV.

I don't remember what we watched or even what we talked about. I just recall the fuzzy feeling I began to experience after the fourth can of beer and how I wasn't thirsty anymore. Clara turned toward me shortly thereafter.

"Do you ever want it?" she asked.

She was so close that her eyes merged, or maybe it was the effect of the beer that made them look that way. "Did anyone ever tell you how pretty you are?" I said.

She giggled, and I focused on her mouth, then did something incredulous. I kissed her. I expected her to push me away in anger. Instead, she thrust her tongue in my mouth. Her breath came in swift little gasps.

What experimenting I'd done had been with boys or alone. This was a whole new ball game, and as amazed as I was that this was happening, I was more astonished at my own excitement.

Clara, though, seemed to know what do. I attributed it to instinct or something that Dean had taught her. She slid a hand in my panties, and I stiffened with shock. Her fingers were warm, the touch so tantalizing it was almost painful.

"Come on," she said softly. "Let's get out of our clothes."

That first touch of breasts I never forgot. Clara's were full, her belly rounded. I pressed against her, aware of skin the texture of dry silk, of warm lips and tongue, of her urgent touch that was quickly bringing me to orgasm.

She took my hand, put it between her spread legs and moved my fingers against her, pushing them inside every few strokes, moaning and whispering — "faster, faster" — until she shuddered in climax.

We spent the next few days in a state of arousal. When driven dazedly outside by hunger, we watched each other eat as if the act of shoveling food in our mouths was lustful, then we hurried back to the tangle of sheets we'd left behind. At the end of three days we ran out of money.

We were both expelled, of course. My parents drove the four hundred miles to retrieve me and my belongings. It was a silent trip home, and, once there, I lost touch with Clara and myself.

"How did you find me?" I asked.

Clara appeared heavier, but the extra weight

agreed with her. It softened her, adding to her womanly appearance. Although her eyes looked as fawnlike as in her youth, gray streaked her hair. "I saw your name and address in the *Alumnus*."

I remember giving an old college friend — the same one who told me Clara married Dean the spring after our dismissal — permission to put them in the magazine. "It's been a long time. What brings you here?"

"You," she said with a smile that drew my attention to her mouth. "I'm between jobs, divorced; the kids have fled the nest. You always told me how wonderful your state was. Thought I'd give it a try."

Returning the smile, I said, "Do you have a place to stay?"

"Not yet."

"You do now."

I gave her the address and directions to my small house, told her I'd be home at five-thirty. After work, I briskly showed her the guest bedroom, the bathroom. Then I heated up leftovers for dinner.

At the table I looked up and saw her watching me eat. I put my fork down. "What is it?"

"I never forgot," she said.

I took a deep breath. "I tried. It would come back to me at odd times." And always with an almost electric thrill. "Those few days set off repercussions that echoed for twenty-eight years."

"I know," she admitted.

"Maybe I should have listened to what I was feeling," I mused aloud.

"I don't regret the kids," she said. "They were

worth it. But there comes a time when I can no longer ignore who I am and what I want."

I stared at her, feeling strangely agitated and a little afraid, but not at all confused. I knew exactly what I wanted. She was sitting across the table.

Never Too Late

Frankie J. Jones

Grandma, let's double-date tonight."

Amelia grinned as she slid the last of the dinner's leftovers into the refrigerator.

"I'd love to, Danny, but to double-date I'd have to have a date. I assume it still works that way."

"Minor detail," Danny, her seventeen-year-old grandson, said with a shrug. "We'll go over to the strip. Lots of gay men and lesbians hang out over there."

Amelia laughed and shook her had. "I doubt you'll find many old lesbians 'hanging out.' "

Jenny, Amelia's fifteen-year-old granddaughter, came into the kitchen in time to hear Amelia's last comment. "You're not old, Grandma."

"I'm seventy-two," Amelia reminded her.

"When I'm seventy-two, I hope I have half your energy," Amelia's daughter-in-law added as she came in with a handful of dirty plates. "It's your turn for dishes, Danny."

"Oh, Mom. I did them last night."

"To pay me back for taking your turn on Saturday night," Jenny reminded him.

Danny rolled his eyes and reached for the things his mom held.

Amelia and Laura retired to the living room, and Jenny went upstairs to do her homework.

Amelia glanced at the clock over the fireplace. "Does Bill work this late often?" she asked as she settled onto the couch.

Laura sat in a recliner across from her. "No, it's just for this special project he's working on." She popped the footrest up and snuggled in. "How are you doing with all of this?" she asked, referring to the devastating flood that had forced Amelia from her home.

Amelia sighed. "Everyone has been great. I'm so thankful I had time to take out the things that mattered most to me. I can't bear to think about those poor people who lost everything." She smoothed her short gray hair back. "I love you, but in all honesty I will be glad to get back into my own home. Everyone has been wonderful, but —"

Laura held up her hand. "You don't have to explain to me. I know how you feel. But you're welcome here as long as you'd like to stay."

"Thanks. And I really am enjoying spending time with the kids. They're growing up so fast."

The doorbell interrupted them.

"Who could that be?" Amelia wondered out loud.

Laura kicked the footrest down and hopped up. "I forgot to tell you." She scurried toward the door and called over her shoulder, "I invited the next-door neighbor over for cake and coffee. I hope you don't mind."

Before Amelia could respond, Laura disappeared into the foyer. Amelia wondered if it would be inexcusably rude to go upstairs. She wasn't in the mood to chitchat with a stranger. The subject of the flooding was sure to come up, and Amelia didn't want to discuss it any further; that was all anyone could talk about.

Laura returned with a short, slender woman dressed in a black jogging suit and brilliant white sneakers.

"Amelia, this is our neighbor Caroline Donner. Caroline, this is my mother-in-law, Amelia Werner."

The woman who appeared to be in her mid-to-late sixties extended her hand. It was warm and soft, and without warning Amelia felt a delicious tingle start in the bottom of her stomach as she returned Caroline's firm grip. As she gazed into mischievous gray eyes, it occurred to her that maybe she shouldn't go upstairs after all.

Throughout the evening, Amelia found her gaze lingering on Caroline, until she finally had to scold herself for her foolish thoughts. After all, she was seventy-two. It was too late in the game for her to start thinking like this. She'd had her share of flings in her younger days and had had seventeen wonderful years with Suzy. A small stab of pain pricked her at the thought of Suzy. It had been almost eight years since Suzy had left her for a woman half their age. She pushed the thoughts away when she realized Caroline was standing up to leave. Amelia found herself following Caroline and Laura to the door.

"It was nice to meet you," Caroline said and extended her hand to Amelia.

"Yes," Amelia answered as she again enjoyed the feel of Caroline's hand in hers.

"I'm sure we'll see each other again before you return home," Caroline assured her as she reached for the doorknob.

"Caroline," Laura piped in. "Amelia loves flowers, and I noticed in the newspaper today that there's going to be an orchid show at Central Park Mall tomorrow. Maybe you two would like to attend."

Amelia couldn't stop the small gasp of shock that escaped her. How could Laura be so bold?

"I love orchids," Caroline said as she gave a small smirk. She turned to Amelia. "Is it a date?"

Amelia felt like a stammering teenager. "Um, sure," she managed.

"I'll call you tomorrow, and we can decide what time to leave then." Caroline was gone before Amelia could reply.

* * * * *

The flower show turned out to be not only fragrant and beautiful, but informative as well. Caroline kept Amelia fascinated with details about the different varieties and the care required of the delicate flowers. After viewing the show they stopped by the food court for a beer.

Caroline took a long drink and swallowed slowly. Amelia found herself smiling at the look of enjoyment on Caroline's face.

"I don't think I've ever seen anyone savor a swallow of beer so completely."

Caroline leaned forward and said in a conspiratorial whisper, "This is the first beer I've had in fifteen months."

"Oh dear, I hope I'm not the evil influence that sent you over the edge," Amelia teased.

Caroline tilted her head and grinned. "I've no doubt that you could be an evil influence, but my doctor is the reason for my abstinence. She worries about every little thing I do." Caroline took another sip and sighed. "It's hell getting old, isn't it?"

Amelia shrugged. "I've learned to adjust to the changes. I move a little slower, hold a book slightly closer and turn the TV up a tad louder, but I cope."

Caroline shook her head. "It's the nights that kill me. Those little spurts of sleep I get in between the twenty thousand trips to the bathroom. And that hour-long ritual in the morning of putting my body back on — my teeth, my eyes and my ears."

"I didn't know you wore a hearing aid," Amelia said, unconsciously speaking a little louder.

Caroline waved her hand. "I don't. I just like to bitch."

Suddenly they were laughing uncontrollably. After several seconds, Amelia wiped her eyes and took a deep breath.

"I'll bet everyone is gawking at us," Caroline said as she, too, wiped away tears. "They're over there feeling sorry for a couple of old drunk women."

Amelia picked up her beer bottle. "Here's to old women everywhere. May they all know the laughter we just shared."

The days flew by with Amelia and Caroline spending many hours together. Amelia heard from the contractor who was repairing her house in Victoria. He anticipated that the repairs would be completed within the next three weeks. She found herself torn between being anxious to return home and sad at the thought of her time with Caroline ending.

She packed a thermos of iced tea into the picnic basket and pushed the thoughts away. It wasn't like Victoria was *that* far from San Antonio. She and Caroline would simply visit each other. She grabbed the picnic basket and headed toward Caroline's house.

Caroline met her at the door. "Have a seat. I'm almost ready," she assured Amelia as she motioned her toward the sofa.

Amelia stood beside Caroline and smiled. "It's a perfect day for a picnic."

Caroline gazed at her. "There's only one thing could make it better," she stated.

"What's that?"

"This." Caroline leaned forward and kissed Amelia softly.

Amelia's breath caught as a herd of butterflies stampeded through her stomach.

"I've been wanting to do that for so long," Caroline admitted.

"Why did you wait so long?" Amelia asked as she brushed back a stray lock of Caroline's hair.

"I kept telling myself that you would be leaving soon, so what purpose would it serve to get something started?"

"What changed your mind?"

Caroline stared into her eyes. "I realized you really would be leaving soon and if I didn't take the chance, I'd never know what it would have been like to have kissed you."

Amelia leaned toward her. "Was it worth a second try?"

Caroline smiled and ran her hand over Amelia's cheek. "I think we should try it several more times, just to be sure."

"Sounds like an excellent idea to me."

Their lips met softly but grew more insistent as the kiss lengthened and intensified. Caroline's hands ran over the back of Amelia's thin, cotton shirt.

"If you're going to kiss me like that, I'm going to have to sit down," Amelia said.

Caroline led her to the sofa where her lips once more began their investigative journey over Amelia's face and neck.

Amelia moaned her appreciation as she nibbled Caroline's ear. A current of desire shot through her as Caroline's hand moved around to cup her breast and gently squeeze the nipple.

"Do you need all of these clothes?" Caroline asked.

"I think we both could do without them," Amelia agreed. They slowly undressed each other.

"You're beautiful," they both whispered at the same time and broke into laughter.

Their laughter was halted when Amelia's hand slipped up Caroline's side and began to tease an already taut nipple. Their lips met in a wave of desire that shook both of them.

Caroline pushed Amelia back until they were stretched out side by side. Her lips slowly traveled down Amelia's body, totally indifferent, it seemed, to the fact that the skin wasn't quite as toned and smooth as it had once been, or that her body wasn't as flexible as it had been twenty years earlier.

Age and flexibility were forgotten when Caroline's tongue slipped between Amelia's legs. As the waves of pleasure washed over Amelia, a fleeting thought brought a smile to her lips. It was never too late for love.

About the Authors

LAURA ADAMS — Laura Adams is the no longer closely guarded *nom de plume* of Karin Kallmaker. As Karin's supernatural and science-fiction loving alter-ego, "Laura's" works for Naiad include *Night Vision, Christabel,* and *The Dawning.*

SAXON BENNETT lives in Phoenix, Arizona, with her loving partner and furry pet pal. She is still learning a lot about her favorite subject which, of course, would be lesbians and wishes someday we might have our own planet when the human race moves about the universe. Until then, she is content with her family and friends and hopes to hold many a picnic in nirvana. She is the author of *The Wish List, Old Ties, A Question of Love,* and her new novel, *Both Sides.*

DIANA TREMAIN BRAUND, a former college professor, lives and works on the Maine coast. Her first novel, *The Way Life Should Be,* was published in 1998, and her second novel, *Wicked Good Time,* was published in the summer of 1999.

JACKIE CALHOUN considers herself lucky to have enjoyed the best of two worlds but is happiest in this one, where she writes full-time and lives with her other half, Diane Mandler, along the Fox River in Wisconsin, only an hour from her lake cottage. Having raised two daughters, she now has two granddaughters. Calhoun's interests include reading, classical music and the environment. She is the author of ten books published by Naiad, including *Birds of a Feather* (1999), and has stories in several Naiad anthologies.

KATE CALLOWAY was born in 1957. She has published several novels with Naiad including *First Impressions, Second Fiddle, Third Degree, Fourth Down, Fifth Wheel, Sixth Sense,* and *Seventh Heaven,* in the Cassidy James mystery series. Kate's stories are in *Lady Be Good* and *Dancing in the Dark.* Her hobbies include cooking, winetasting, boating, songwriting and spending time with Carol. She currently splits her time between Southern California and the Pacific Northwest, setting for the Cassidy James novels.

CHRISTINE CASSIDY, the eldest of six children, grew up in Upstate New York on Lake Ontario. She is an editor for Naiad Press and also works in publishing in New York City, where she lives with Nan Kinney, "professional lesbian" extraordinaire. With gratitude to Michael Cunningham for his inspiration, this is her first story published by Naiad.

LYN DENISON was a librarian before becoming a full-time writer. Her partner of eleven years is also a librarian, which goes to prove that tidying books is not all that goes on between library shelves. Lyn lives with her partner in a historic inner city suburb in Brisbane, the capital city of Queensland, Australia's Sunshine State. Apart from writing she loves reading, talking about books, cross-stitching and modern country music. Occasionally she ventures out line dancing, which even she will admit is not a pretty sight.

CATHERINE ENNIS is a Southerner by birth and still lives in the deep south with her long-time lover and an assortment of pets. She has enjoyed many pastimes, including gardening, gourmet cooking, fishing, and working on her Model A Ford coupe. Catherine's books are set in the locales with which she is most familiar: the New Orleans area, the Memphis–Nashville area and the Louisiana Cajun country. Her early work experience included wholesale florist and research office manager, medical illustrator and teacher, followed by some years on the arts and crafts show circuit. Finally she started her own business utilizing her art background, making her work even more enjoyable because, obviously, no one could have a better boss. Writing has become her favorite hobby.

PENNY HAYES was born in Johnson City, New York, February 10, 1940. As a child she lived on a farm near Binghamton, New York. She later attended college in Utica and Buffalo, New York, and in Huntington, West Virginia, graduating with degrees in art, nursery school education, and elementary and special education. She is retired from public school teaching and now devotes her time to writing and anything to do with the outdoors and good conversation. Her novels include *The Long Trail, Yellowthroat, Montana Feathers, Grassy Flats, Kathleen O'Donald, Now and Then, City Lights/Country Candles,* and most recently *Omaha's Bell.* She has also written short stories for *The Erotic Naiad, The Romantic Naiad, The Mysterious Naiad, The First Time Ever, Dancing in the Dark, Lady Be Good, The Touch of Your Hand,* and *The Very Thought of You.*

PEGGY J. HERRING lives on seven acres of mesquite in South Texas. She is the author of *Once More with Feeling, Love's Harvest, Hot Check, A Moment's Indiscretion, Those Who Wait,* and *To Have and To Hold.* In addition, she has contributed to the Naiad anthologies *The First Time Ever, Dancing in the Dark, Lady Be Good, The Touch of Your Hand,* and *The Very Thought of You.*

LINDA HILL is living happily-ever-after near Boston with her partner of ten years and their two pups, Molly and Maggie. Her novels include *Never Say Never, Class*

Reunion, Just Yesterday, and *Change of Heart.* Her short stories have also appeared in several of the Naiad anthologies, including *Dancing in the Dark, Lady Be Good, The Touch of Your Hand,* and *The Very Thought of You.* She promises a fourth romance novel in the fall of 2000.

BARBARA JOHNSON spends her free time prowling various state fairs looking for Brett Higgins. She's not entirely convinced the woman is only the figment of someone's imagination. When not prowling, she has written four full-length novels for Naiad — *Stonehurst, The Beach Affair, Bad Moon Rising,* and *Strangers in the Night* — in addition to several short stories.

FRANKIE J. JONES lives in San Antonio, Texas. She is the author of *Rhythm Tide, Whispers in the Wind,* and *Captive Heart.*

KARIN KALLMAKER was born in 1960 and raised by her loving, middle-class parents in California's Central Valley. The physician's Statement of Live Birth plainly states "Sex: Female" and "Cry: Lusty." Both are still true. From a normal childhood and equally unremarkable public school adolescence, she went on to obtain an ordinary bachelor's degree from the California State University at Sacramento. At the age of sixteen, eyes wide open, she fell into the arms of her first and only sweetheart. Ten years later, after seeing the film *Desert Hearts,* her sweetheart descended on the Berkeley Public Library determined to find some of "those" books. "Rule, Jane" led to "Lesbianism — Fiction" and then on to book after

self-affirming book by and about lesbians. These books
were the encouragement Karin needed to forget the so-
called "mainstream" and spin her first romance for
lesbians. That manuscript became her first Naiad Press
book, *In Every Port.* She now lives in the San Francisco
Bay Area with that very same sweetheart; she is a
one-woman woman. The happily-ever-after couple celebrated
their twenty-third anniversary in 2000 and are mothers of
two remarkable, amazing, extraordinary children, Kelson
and Eleanor. In addition to *In Every Port,* she has
authored the best-selling *Touchwood, Paperback Romance,
Car Pool, Painted Moon, Wild Things, Embrace in Motion,
Making Up for Lost Time, Watermark,* and the forthcoming
Unforgettable. She also writes for Naiad Press as Laura
Adams.

JANET McCLELLAN, author of the Naiad Press mystery
series featuring Kansas City, Missouri, Police Department
detective Tru North, has more than twenty-five years of
criminal justice experience. She has contributed to two
previous Naiad anthologies, *Lady Be Good* and *The Touch
of Your Hand.* After years in law enforcement in the
midwest, Janet has finally been able to move in a truly
northern fashion, and now lives in Oregon. She takes long
walks on the beach with her faithful German shepherd,
Trooper, and thinks of ways to weave fact into fiction.

MARIANNE MARTIN is the author of the best-selling
novels *Legacy of Love, Love in the Balance, Dawn of the
Dance,* and *Never Ending.* Among her varied careers,
Marianne has been a public school teacher, a

photojournalist, and MHSAA basketball and softball coach, a collegiate field hockey coach, and a photographer. She has been active in athletics since childhood, and has played and coached ASA fast-pitch softball for many years. Her other hobbies include building and remodeling, drawing, landscaping, and of course, reading. Her short stories can be found in several Naiad anthologies, *Lady Be Good, The Touch of Your Hand,* and *The Very Thought of You.*

ANN O'LEARY's career began in film production and, except for a brief youthful and misguided dalliance with life as a restaurateur, it has been focused on advertising. After several years working as a TV producer in ad agencies, Ann and her talented sound engineer partner opened an audio production studio producing TV soundtracks. Having traveled extensively, Ann is happily settled with her partner in Melbourne, Australia, where she was born. Sharing their wild garden with rainbow lorikeets and brushtail possums, they live in an area affectionately known as "dyke city," nestled between mountains and bay beaches, a few miles from the center of Melbourne. When not out enjoying the restaurants and cafés for which Melbourne is famous, Ann spends much of her time writing, and is the author of *Letting Go, Julia's Song,* and *The Other Woman.*

TRACEY RICHARDSON's short stories have appeared in *The Touch of Your Hand, Lady Be Good, Dancing in the Dark,* and *The Very Thought of You.* Her first novel for Naiad was the romance *Northern Blue,* published in 1996. Her mystery, *Last Rites,* was published in 1997, followed by

Over the Line in 1998. Her latest mystery novel, published by Naiad Press in 1999, is *Double Takeout.* Tracey and her partner, Sandra, live in Ontario, Canada.

LISA SHAPIRO is the author of *The Color of Winter, Sea to Shining Sea,* and *Endless Love,* as well as short stories in several Naiad anthologies. She and her beloved partner, Lynne D'Orsay, together for thirteen years, now live and enjoy the sunshine, the river, coffee and grits in Tampa, Florida.

THERESE SZYMANSKI — Little did she know that opening the perfume-scented envelope that came in the mail one day would lead to a rather steamy elevator sex-scene with a woman she had never met. She plans to finally meet Barbara Johnson soon, although friends have sworn not to let them anywhere near any elevators. Therese is the author of Brett Higgins' mysteries *When the Dancing Stops, When the Dead Speak,* and *When Some Body Disappears.*

JULIA WATTS, a native of southeastern Kentucky, is a part-time teacher, a part-time nanny, and a rest-of-the-time writer. Her story "Four Letters" was drawn from her fascination with the American woman who discovered freedom in the factories while the men were fighting World War II. Julia is the author of four novels published by Naiad Press: *Wildwood Flowers, Phases of the Moon, Piece of My Heart,* and *Wedding Bell Blues.*

LAURA DeHART YOUNG currently has five romance novels published with Naiad Press: *There Will Be No Goodbyes, Family Secrets, Love on the Line, Private Passions,* and her newest book, *Intimate Strangers.* When not writing for Naiad, Laura works as a communications manager for a worldwide information company. She lives in Atlanta, Georgia, with her pug, Dudley.

LOOKING FOR NAIAD?

**Buy our books at
www.naiadpress.com**

**or call our toll-free number
1-800-533-1973**

**or by fax (24 hours a day)
1-850-539-9731**

A few of the publications of
THE NAIAD PRESS, INC.
P.O. Box 10543   Tallahassee, Florida 32302
Phone (850) 539-5965
Toll-Free Order Number: 1-800-533-1973
Web Site: WWW.NAIADPRESS.COM
Mail orders welcome. Please include 15% postage.
Write or call for our free catalog which also features an
incredible selection of lesbian videos.

THE VERY THOUGHT OF YOU edited by Barbara Grier and
Christine Cassidy. 288 pp. Erotic love stories by Naiad Press
authors.   ISBN 1-56280-250-X $14.95

TO HAVE AND TO HOLD by Petty J. Herring. 192 pp. Their
friendship grows to intense passion . . .   ISBN 1-56280-251-8   11.95

INTIMATE STRANGER by Laura DeHart Young. 192 pp.
Ignoring Tray's myserious past, could Cole be playing with fire?
                                             ISBN 1-56280-249-6   11.95

SHATTERED ILLUSIONS by Kaye Davis. 256 pp. 4th
Maris Middleton mystery.   ISBN 1-56280-252-6   11.95

SETUP by Claire McNab. 224 pp. 11th Detective Inspector Carol
Ashton mystery.   ISBN 1-56280-255-0   11.95

THE DAWNING by Laura Adams. 224 pp. What if you had the
power to change the past?   ISBN 1-56280-246-1   11.95

NEVER ENDING by Marianne Martin. 224 pp. Temptation
appears in the form of an old friend and lover. ISBN 1-56280-247-X   11.95

ONE OF OUR OWN by Diane Salvatore. 240 pp. Carly Matson
has a secret. So does Lela Johns.   ISBN 1-56280-243-7   11.95

DOUBLE TAKEOUT by Tracey Richardson. 176 pp. 3rd Stevie
Houston mystery.   ISBN 1-56280-244-5   11.95

CAPTIVE HEART by Frankie J. Jones. 176 pp. Love in the
fast lane or heartside romance?   ISBN 1-56280-258-5   11.95

WICKED GOOD TIME by Diana Tremain Braund. 224 pp. In
charge at work, out of control in her heart. ISBN 1-56280-241-0   11.95

SNAKE EYES by Pat Welch. 256 pp. 7th Helen Black mystery.
                                             ISBN 1-56280-242-9   11.95

CHANGE OF HEART by Linda Hill. 176 pp. High fashion and
love in a glamorous world.   ISBN 1-56280-238-0   11.95

WINDROW GARDEN by Janet McClellan. 192 pp. They discover
a passion they never dreamed possible.   ISBN 1-56280-216-X   11.95

PAST DUE by Claire McNab. 224 pp. 10th Carol Ashton
mystery.   ISBN 1-56280-217-8   11.95

CHRISTABEL by Laura Adams. 224 pp. Two captive hearts and
the passion that will set them free.   ISBN 1-56280-214-3   11.95

PRIVATE PASSIONS by Laura DeHart Young. 192 pp. An
unforgettable new portrait of lesbian love . . .   ISBN 1-56280-215-1   11.95

BAD MOON RISING by Barbara Johnson. 208 pp. 2nd Colleen
Fitzgerald mystery.   ISBN 1-56280-211-9   11.95

RIVER QUAY by Janet McClellan. 208 pp. 3rd Tru North
mystery.   ISBN 1-56280-212-7   11.95

ENDLESS LOVE by Lisa Shapiro. 272 pp. To believe, once
again, that love can be forever.   ISBN 1-56280-213-5   11.95

FALLEN FROM GRACE by Pat Welch. 256 pp. 6th Helen Black
mystery.   ISBN 1-56280-209-7   11.95

THE NAKED EYE by Catherine Ennis. 208 pp. Her lover in the
camera's eye . . .   ISBN 1-56280-210-0   11.95

OVER THE LINE by Tracey Richardson. 176 pp. 2nd Stevie
Houston mystery.   ISBN 1-56280-202-X   11.95

JULIA'S SONG by Ann O'Leary. 208 pp. Strangely
disturbing . . . strangely exciting.   ISBN 1-56280-197-X   11.95

LOVE IN THE BALANCE by Marianne K. Martin. 256 pp.
Weighing the costs of love . . .   ISBN 1-56280-199-6   11.95

PIECE OF MY HEART by Julia Watts. 208 pp. All the
stuff that dreams are made of —   ISBN 1-56280-206-2   11.95

MAKING UP FOR LOST TIME by Karin Kallmaker. 240 pp.
Nobody does it better . . .   ISBN 1-56280-196-1   11.95

GOLD FEVER by Lyn Denison. 224 pp. By author of *Dream
Lover.*   ISBN 1-56280-201-1   11.95

WHEN THE DEAD SPEAK by Therese Szymanski. 224 pp. 2nd
Brett Higgins mystery.   ISBN 1-56280-198-8   11.95

FOURTH DOWN by Kate Calloway. 240 pp. 4th Cassidy James
mystery.   ISBN 1-56280-205-4   11.95

A MOMENT'S INDISCRETION by Peggy J. Herring. 176 pp.
There's a fine line between love and lust . . .   ISBN 1-56280-194-5   11.95

CITY LIGHTS/COUNTRY CANDLES by Penny Hayes. 208 pp.
About the women she has known . . .   ISBN 1-56280-195-3   11.95

POSSESSIONS by Kaye Davis. 240 pp. 2nd Maris Middleton
mystery.   ISBN 1-56280-192-9   11.95

A QUESTION OF LOVE by Saxon Bennett. 208 pp. Every
woman is granted one great love.   ISBN 1-56280-205-4   11.95

RHYTHM TIDE by Frankie J. Jones. 160 pp. . . . to desire
passionately and be passionately desired.   ISBN 1-56280-189-9   11.95

PENN VALLEY PHOENIX by Janet McClellan. 208 pp. 2nd
Tru North Mystery.   ISBN 1-56280-200-3   11.95

BY RESERVATION ONLY by Jackie Calhoun. 240 pp. A
chance for true happiness.   ISBN 1-56280-191-0   11.95

OLD BLACK MAGIC by Jaye Maiman. 272 pp. 9th Robin
Miller mystery.   ISBN 1-56280-175-9   11.95

LEGACY OF LOVE by Marianne K. Martin. 240 pp. Women
will do anything for her . . .   ISBN 1-56280-184-8   11.95

LETTING GO by Ann O'Leary. 160 pp. Laura, at 39, in love
with 23-year-old Kate.   ISBN 1-56280-183-X   11.95

LADY BE GOOD edited by Barbara Grier and Christine Cassidy.
288 pp. Erotic stories by Naiad Press authors.   ISBN 1-56280-180-5   14.95

CHAIN LETTER by Claire McNab. 288 pp. 9th Carol Ashton
mystery.   ISBN 1-56280-181-3   11.95

NIGHT VISION by Laura Adams. 256 pp. Erotic fantasy romance
by "famous" author.   ISBN 1-56280-182-1   11.95

SEA TO SHINING SEA by Lisa Shapiro. 256 pp. Unable to resist
the raging passion . . .   ISBN 1-56280-177-5   11.95

THIRD DEGREE by Kate Calloway. 224 pp. 3rd Cassidy James
mystery.   ISBN 1-56280-185-6   11.95

WHEN THE DANCING STOPS by Therese Szymanski. 272 pp.
1st Brett Higgins mystery.   ISBN 1-56280-186-4   11.95

PHASES OF THE MOON by Julia Watts. 192 pp. . . . . hungry
for everything life has to offer.   ISBN 1-56280-176-7   11.95

BABY IT'S COLD by Jaye Maiman. 256 pp. 5th Robin Miller
mystery.   ISBN 1-56280-156-2   10.95

CLASS REUNION by Linda Hill. 176 pp. The girl from her
past . . .   ISBN 1-56280-178-3   11.95

DREAM LOVER by Lyn Denison. 224 pp. A soft, sensuous,
romantic fantasy.   ISBN 1-56280-173-1   11.95

FORTY LOVE by Diana Simmonds. 288 pp. Joyous, heart-
warming romance.   ISBN 1-56280-171-6   11.95

These are just a few of the many Naiad Press titles — we are the oldest and
largest lesbian/feminist publishing company in the world. We also offer an
enormous selection of lesbian video products. Please request a complete
catalog. We offer personal service; we encourage and welcome direct mail
orders from individuals who have limited access to bookstores carrying our
publications.